#Dead*Things*

A Novel

#Dead*Things*

A Novel

Book One

By Reese *Riley*

Corona Sky Productions, Inc.

#DeadThings, A Novel

This edition published by Corona Sky Productions. For information address Corona Sky Productions New York, New York.

First Edition

Library of Congress Cataloging-in-Publication Data

Reese, Riley, 1987 –

www.ReeseRiley.com

@ReeseRileyCSP

@CoronaSkyProd

ISBN 978-0615669205

Manufactured in the United States of America

Praise to God for blessing me with the gift of storytelling. For a second, I questioned the gift that you bestowed upon me –never again will I question anything you have given me. My mother, sisters, and brother. My extended family, especially *Ophelia* –this is specifically for you.

For *Vanne* and *Darryll* –your creative input helped shape this dream I had into fruition. *Jordan* and *Chel* –my neighbors up North, love you much, *eh. Marcus* I have watched you grow and prosper as an actor and blossom into a truly spiritual man, stay the same.

This Book is Dedicated to the Memory of Trayvon Martin, May justice be served at last

#JusticeForTrayvon

#SheIsLove

She lives in a glass house all alone

From her ivory towers, she throws stones,

Pebbles, rocks, and bricks,

She beckons me tauntingly with a kiss,

But she is void of compassion,

She is obliteration and devastation ,

She is cloaked in tragedy and disillusion

I am enveloped in her maddening confusion –but she just laughs…

She is my heart, my breath, my mind,

My trinity –my divinity

She is the ultimate contradiction,

She chases away my gray with storm clouds and typhoons

Leaving me entombed in her,

Basking in the beautiful essence that is her,

She is love.

-*Reese Riley*

#Dead*Things A Novel By Reese Riley*

Per the Publisher request, no introduction will be need.

Chapter

1

You gotta love the future. In the future maps are no longer needed; a GPS can locate any burger joint, bank, or sex shop in the area. Social networks keep friends from middle school connected via invisible beams of light that carries data all over the world. If first came The Word and God was the creator of that *Word*, then Man was coming in a close second with the internet.

You gotta love words. Words can build a person up, but words can also tear a person asunder. Sometimes, words can cause pleasure.

His cell phone vibrated. Ken immediately picked up his smart phone and opened the app, *GrindR*. The App was designed for gay men to meet up; a hook up app.

Ken was nineteen and in his second semester of college. Manhattan City College commute was over an hour drive, but provided Ken with all the culture and snobbery he has grown to love about the Big Apple.

Even though Ken was blessed with good looks, his self image has always been distorted. Coming to terms with his own homosexuality was quite a mission. He had yet to even get a kiss from a guy let alone hook up.

In 2012, the world had become so reliant on their smart phones and apps, people forgot how to actually date.

"When are we meeting?" RedRangerRyan asked via the app's instant massager.

Not one to beat-around-the-bush and really wanting to finally meet up with the very handsome Red Ranger, Ken shot back quickly. "Let's make it 7:00pm."

A smile crept on Ken's face; the ease of it all seemed criminally simple. Ken pondered on all the consequences that were related to this rendezvous, but the rewards were too impressive not to tempt fate.

Ken fumbled with his lighter as he attempted to light up his Newport. He made a muted curse as the meddlesome winds blew out his flame. When the cigarette was finally lit, Ken took in a small puff. Ken watched the sky begin to change to indigo as the sun sank behind the stone and steel buildings.

Brooklyn was colder than usual. Ken already fair Irish complexion looked even more sallow than usual. His lips were in a pout as he puffed on his Newport. His lanky six feet and one inch form was hunched over, shivering from the unseasonably cold April night. His iceberg blue eyes scanned across the park where he was to meet Ryan. His brown hair was covered by a black fedora.

"Ken," a voice called out.

Ken immediately turned around, halfway expecting Ryan to look nothing like his picture. But he did. He looked just like he did online; blonde, strong German build, slightly shorter than Ken. The baritone in his voice made Ken smile organically.

"Afraid you wouldn't show," Ken said with a smile.

"What would give you an idea like that?" Ryan made a quick scan of the area before suggesting, "Let's go for a walk."

During the walk Ken unloaded about his school life and his numerous challenges with his sexuality. Ryan used his active listening skills during Ken's monologue. The two walked deeper into the borough and the sun became less and less visible.

After aimlessly following Ryan Ken finally asked, "Where are we going?"

"Just a little further," Ryan said as he texted with his smart phone.

Ken was not very familiar with Brooklyn, and his spider senses were telling him something was terribly wrong with this entire scenario. But he could not come off as a pussy. That would assure he would not get laid. Ryan was hot and not getting laid would no bullshit.

Ken walked with Ryan into an urban neighborhood. It was somewhat empty and isolated.

"I gotta take a leak," Ryan announced. "What about you?"

Not sure if that was code for sex Ken replied, "Yeah."

The two men walk into the alley and went behind a large green dumpster. Ryan begins to unbuckle his pants and Ken did the same. Then an unexpected force pushes Ken to the ground;

disoriented Ken attempted to regain his poise but was again knocked down by another shove.

Ken face hit the pavement; dust and gravel was sucked into his nose and mouth. Then a boot collided with his rib cage. Again. And again. And again.

"*What the fuck are you doing?*" Ryan squealed in a high nasally fashion. "We were supposed just scare him."

The other assailants paid no attention to Ryan's objection as the continued to pound, kick, and choke Ken. Ken face was covered in welts and blood, his body tendered from a barrage of attacks.

Ken saw them, all three of them. One was a black kid, no older than twenty one, slim but strong build, with a sucker in his mouth as he kicked Ken in the ribs.

The second was a white male, approximately the same age as the other, and had a slightly more rounded shaved head. He had tattoos that were etched across his neck. He rummaged through Ken's pockets in search for cash.

"Fucking watch it," the round male said. "You almost fucking kicked me, Sam."

Sam cut his eyes at him with anger. "No fucking names, yo!"

Ryan just watched. Ken could see the confliction in his eyes. Ryan knew everything about this was wrong. This was not how it was supposed to go down. They were just supposed to rob and scare him.

Ken laid there, barely conscious but lucid enough to feel pain. Sam squatted down to Ken who lay on his back looking up at Sam. With an iron-cold, sociopathic grip, Sam craned Ken closer to him. Ken could smell the cherry flavored sucker on Sam's breath.

"Fucking faggot," hissed Sam. Sam dug into his pocket and removed a small pocket knife then with lightening speed he penetrated Ken's stomach.

Sam allowed Ken's body to fall to the ground mercilessly. The boys then dispersed. Ken sat there bleeding and waiting to die.

Death. Dying is not something that is smooth. You would think, after millions of years of practice The Grim Reaper would have this down to a science. Death first takes the wind out of the body; strips all the fight from the spirit.

Death drags the soul down lower and deeper into its abyss; an abyss that very few people ever return from. But some of us get a reprieve; some of us – the truly *lucky* ones- get a second chance. "Are you alright?" a soft female voice said. The voice echoed and bounced around Ken's mind.

Ken could not see her face; his eyes were too swollen from the bruises. His voice was gargled by blood. But he could see that she was incandescent; her skin shone as it absorbed the light of the moon.

"You'll be dead soon if you don't get some help," the female voice said. "Luckily, I'm a doctor."

She kneeled down over his dying body. She ever so gently lifted his head and began to cradle it. Her body shivered as she began to rock back and forth making mousy whimpering.

She felt like steel. Cold and smooth and without... depth. He felt like he was held by something soulless; like a gorgeous mannequin with a porcelain china face.

The female lifted Ken up close to her slender body. She whispers how she plans to save his life and there was nothing to fear. She could feel it grow within her; the hunger. She smiles at him innocently right before she sinks her dagger-like fangs into his throat. The Bite only lasted a second before she pulled away.

Somehow Ken could finally see out of his eyes again. It was if the crimson colored clouds were pushed away by the wind. She was that wind.

He saw her face. Her face was that of a young Asian female, her mouth was wide and two, thin, feline like fang rested on her bottom lip. Her mouth was kissed with splashes of blood. Her long black hair snaked down her back. She took her right wrist and took a small bite.

"I will save you, but you must seek vengeance. That is my only requirement."

She elevated his head and hovered her opened wrist above his mouth. Small drops of icy blood fell to Ken's lips. The blood drop onto his tongue; a burning charge shot through him. And like second nature he rose and began to drink from the wound itself.

Then, he blacked out.

Ken was weakened, all groggy from... well he was not sure. Surely he dreamt it all. The night before had to be a nasty acid trip since homophobic beatings and Asian vampiric attacks generally do not happen. At least not all in the same night.

Besides that he did not feel injured. Actually, he felt strong. He felt stronger than he ever felt. He could feel an alien strength course through his muscles. He could hear the faintness of his own heartbeat and the smell of something dead. Something was rotting.

Ken noticed that he was laying in something; it was soft and velvet with cushioning. But it was not comfortable; it felt like he was in a box. It was a coffin.

The fuck?! He Thought. He took his right hand and traced the lacy pattern that lined the casket making sure to pay attention to every grove and pattern.

This is not happening, none of this could have happened, Ken thought.

"Oh but it did," a meek, soft, feminine voice cooed.

Before Ken could rise the vampire pounced; with an unnatural speed to her movements. The vampire's body pinned him to the cushion, her knees locking him into place. Her thin hands pinned Ken's forearms in place.

The incandescent light of the moon shone through the greenhouse where the coffin sat among Jasmine, Evening Primrose, Moon Flowers, and other nocturnal blooming flowers. The aroma of the flowers became even stronger due to Ken's enhanced senses.

"I am Mika, and *I* am you're savior."

The arrogance in her voice was coupled with her girlish innocent and alluring beauty. Her breast were restricted only by her thin crimson rob; teal veins licked through her pale skin.

"Last night you were going to die," Mika began, "until I saved you. Now it is you who must do something for me."

"This isn't real," Ken denied. "This is not real."

"No," Mika hushed Ken, placing a soft kiss on his lips. She took her right hand and grabbed his growing erection. "It is all real," Mika promised.

Mika unfastened his pants and removed his manhood. She then slowly eased her soft nocturnal flower onto him. Ken could feel every sensation coursing through his body.

Her tightness; her smooth satin entrance tightening as her fang began to protrude. Mika rode Ken violently; she took her talon like nails to his face, slashing him violently across the face. Trapped into the erotic moment Ken began to choke Mika, intensifying the experience.

"Kill me," she begged as began to slash her own face. Drop of blood began to fall on Ken's face. The same drops fell on his infant fangs, on his unsuspecting tongue.

Second nature kicked in; well the opposite of nature. Fueled by darkness, an evil, Ken lifted his back from the firmness of the coffin and took a bite in the neck of Mika. Mika released a roaring orgasmic cry.

With a strength that was disproportionate to her size, Mika using one had pinned Ken back to the soft bedding of the coffin.

"We have work to do."And ever so calmly she climbed off; her once bleeding wounds were now closed miraculously and she paid no attention to the feat.

"This isn't without its faults," She said, scanning his brain, reading his thoughts. "These powers can be yours, but you must earn them."

Ken in a shy and somewhat frighten voice asks, "How?"

"In due time," Mika said with a whimsical coo.

"What day is it?" Ken asked as he climbed out of the coffin. He noticed his muscles felt different, he lifted his body as if it was light as vapors. He landed to his feet with a leopard's grace.

"I don't know," Mika said as she fingered the freshly bloomed jasmine. Her index finger stroked the petals with a light brush.

"I have to get home-" Ken said, his mind disoriented, "-I have classes."

Mika let out a demented cackle before refocusing her stone cold eyes on Ken. Her pitying frown; she could not help but find his naive nature amusing.

"I have given you immortality and you're worries about, *school?*" She could not help but to chuckle again. The prospect of one being yanked from the mortal coil, but still be concerned with their formal life was absolutely hilarious.

"Ok," Mika said. "Feel free to see your friends, collect whatever sentimental knickknacks you feel you need.

"But head this warning: you must never reveal yourself to anyone. You risk yourself and us all. Say your goodbyes and meet me back here. You have one hour."

"But I don't even know where I am or how to get back here," Ken protested.

"You're immortal now. You're bound to find your way back to me; I'm your mother after all."

Ken was thirsty. The thirst was like nothing he could ever fathom. But with the thirst there was also hunger; his body felt like it needed everything; food, water, air. This is what being dead feels like; being void of life.

Ken wanted it all of back; but before he could he had to get back to his dorm and pick up his rosary. It belonged to his grandmother who had recently passed. He felt that if he had those beads in his hand he could have her with him.

Then something happen. A cramp in his stomach appeared, grinding his organs as he walked through the congested streets. He held his stomach as he forced his way through the crowds, hoping to find a subway station.

He found something else, Redfield, the street looked familiar. The street began to dawn him in, it was this very street Ryan took to him; the street where he died. Monochromatic replays began to play in Ken's mind.

Ken struggled with staying on task; the memories continued to flood his consciousness. Delirium was beginning to set in; Ken's budding new vampiric powers coupled with his hunger had him confused.

Confused and disoriented, Ken wandered into an alley and his foot stepped into his own dried blood. He was back in the alley. Ken was assaulted with the brutal images all over again; the shock knocked him to his knees.

"No!" He yelled out. His screams filled into the void of the night. Slowly he began to regain his sanity. As his mind began to slowly rematerialize he noticed that his infant fangs were exposed.

Whoa, he thought, and that is when he saw it.

The small red orb stood out surrounded by all the trash in alley that was blanketed by the shadows of night. The baby-vampire walked over to the orb and noticed what it was. It was a sucker.

Fucking faggot the voice echoed in his mind. The voice was as acidic as he remembered. Second nature kicked in; Ken placed the sucker in his mouth and used his pubertal vampire powers.

Ken closed his eyes and when he opened them he was where Sam was; Heavenly Light Baptist Church, in Brooklyn.

The taste of the sucker was revolting. Ken's vampire taste buds completely rebelled against the taste of the sucker. Ken could not taste the artificial cherry flavor created by Man, only the taste of rotting offal.

Ken spat out the candy, the taste was too unpleasant. He got what he needed; he had Sam on his radar now and he knew exactly where to find him. Ken began to run full speed west to the unsuspecting church.

Chapter

2

Deacon Samuel Rishaad Wrinkle made his rounds in the church. There had been recent vandalism by the hoodlum children that lived in the neighborhood. The church had been there since 1951and it was the cornerstone of the East Flatbush neighborhood.

Niggas don't appreciate shit was Sam's philosophy. But what plagued *niggas* was starting to become the last thing on his mind. Sam was moving to Phoenix soon; his fiancé was being station there and he had his fill of Bed-Stuy.

"Are you ready, Samuel," his grandmother asked. The regal ebony skinned woman was wearing sweat pants and a t-shirt; her hands still damp from cleaning.

"Just gotta finish locking up, ma."

Florence was a good grandmother. When Sam's crack addicted mother left in 1995, Florence made sure he was taken care of. She made sure he was loved and that Jesus was always in the home.

Two knocks at the front door. Florence opened the door to see a bloodied teen. Her maternal instincts kicked in.

"Oh my word," she exclaimed. "Come in here, what happen to you?"

Florence scanned the teenage boy looking for any open cuts. She could not see any visible cuts or opened wounds; however his shirt was ripped and stained with blood.

"Samuel," Florence called out, "call the ambulance!"

"No!" the teen cried out. "Don't do that. I-I-I-..."

By now Samuel was already running after his screaming grandmother. Many terrible thoughts ran through his mind in that fraction of a second.

When he made it to his grandmother's church, his heart sank. His eyes met with a phantom. His eyes met with Ken.

The fuck? Sam thought. It was him; the boy he thought should have been in the hospital stood in front of him. He was uninjured and healthy. He was in *his* grandmother's church of all places.

How the fuck he find me here?

His height and body frame took him by surprise; he did not appear as swishy and flimsy as the night before. He stood all six-foot-one; his eyes darkened by his brow. His face smooth and unblemished; showing no signs of the ass whipping he received.

"Sam he needs some help," Florence said franticly, "we need an ambulance."

"No," Ken said in a low acidic growl, "we need a coroner."

With his newly acquired, enhance speed he grabbed Florence by her face, deleting the small space between them.

"Let her go," Sam demanded. "She ain't done shit!"

"*I* didn't do shit," Ken shot back, mocking Sam's urban vernacular. "I don't want her. I want you lover-boy. But you gotta play by the rules."

The darkness that lives in vampires had taken over Ken so greatly that his manhood hardened. Giving into darkness is always sexy. The magic and sex appeal of a vampire has already been documented. Even the mythical Dracula has displayed this power over fair maidens who easily succumbed to his powers.

Ken was no different. Giving into this force was too intoxicating, too empowering. He went from being another ameba in the vast cosmic ocean to the King of the Sea. The power was like nothing a human could ever know. And it coursed through is blood.

He was in charge of the highest authority right. The authority that is usually in the hands of God only; he had the power to chose who lived and died.

Sam positioned his body as if he was going to suddenly attack the vampire. In response Ken tightened his grip, his nails now cutting into Florence skin.

The warm of her touched him. Instinct took over and he snatched his hands away. Ken began to taste his fingers. The sweet nectar tickled his tongue with sparkling delight. His eyes rolled in the back of his head. His head was out of the game for a second and Sam tackled him.

Sam mounted him and delivered a series of punches to Ken's face. His fist collided seven times against his cold face as Ken feeble sucked his fingers.

Ken could feel the attack, it was not painless, but his pain could not equate to the delight that was in the blood that his fingers only had morsels of.

Using his hands Ken shoved Sam of his of him and with the same momentum jumped to his feet. Sam pulled out the small knife; Ken could smell his lingering mortal blood on the tactical folding knife.

"Give that to me," Ken demanded.

"Oh I'll give it to you, faggot," Sam said as he sized up Ken while pointing the blade at him.

This was it. Someone had to die. More appropriately someone was about to die now. Armed with his trusty knife Sam charged. Curious to learn the extent of his new powers, Ken tried to stop the knife with his palm.

The blade sliced through his hand sending pain throughout his body. "FUCK!" he cried as his fangs appeared, with one punch Sam was sent many feet backwards.

"Look at the mess you made," Mika said. Her tiny Asian frame covered by tight dark jeans and knee high heeled boots that matched her ruffled crimson blouse.

"How did you find me?" Ken asked Mika.

"Same way you found him," Mika said. "Don't let me interrupt. Carry on. Me and Flo' will have a little *'girls only'* talk."

Mika bashfully smiled pulling a crying Florence to her feet. "Come on Flo, let's talk make-up."

"Mama!" Sam screamed as he tried to run over to Florence who cried out for her grandson. He was snatched in mid-run by Ken. Ken held him from behind and with great force he penetrated his throat with his teeth.

The taste of Sam's blood was even sweeter than the tiny drops of Florence's blood. Sam cried out, his eyes locked with Florence who mooed in horror at her grandson's plight.

Ken held on to Sam sloppily and Sam took the small knife and stabbed Ken his left thigh. And with that Sam was freed. He ran over to Mika and attempted to stab her.

The ancient vampire caught him by his wrist and craned him close to her face. She had no breath, which was the first thing Sam noticed.

"How *dare* you," Mika said with utter disgust. "Where were you raised? Think you can just *shank* all your problems away."

Ken began to slowly heal. "How you feeling over there *Barbie*," Mika said, still holding Sam in her talons.

"*Barbie?*" Ken asked.

"What, you don't like it," she asked; eyes still lock in total sync with Sam's.

"Not particularly," he said, tone dripped with sarcasm.

"We're leaving," Mika said. "I believe we've over stayed our welcome."

"I still have to kill him," Ken said, his voice was monotone, lacking any emotion.

"Nah," Mika said. "He has balls, especially for a mortal. Unfortunately, when I was mortal, I used to slice them off."

Mika smiled darkly, "Yo, Flo! Come here." Florence rose to her feet but did not move closer to the vampire. "Don't worry, Flo. Not to sound cliché, but if I wanted you dead, you would have been tipped off by me bisecting your breast.

"So kindly bring your buns over here," Mika said sweetly. Her voice was like honey, it dripped sugary politeness but the evil that was very apparent made her all the more frightening.

Florence slowly walked over to Mika very cautiously. Mika could smell her fear, she could hear Florence's heart race. She became excited and her thin fangs appeared.

"Don't worry Samuel," Mika said mockingly. "Neither Ken nor I will kill anyone. Besides, you're the *true* murder aren't you?"

A smile appeared on her lovely porcelain face. Using Sam's own hand she forced the knife in Florence's heart. Florence's blood spurted from her mouth onto the blade and Sam's now bloodied hand.

"May I?" Mika asked. With her free hand Mika dug in Sam's pocket and pulled out a small phone.

"Fuck, I love a good tragedy," Mika said before punching Sam into the vast amount of pews in the church.

Ken growled at Sam as he was about to pounce. "No," Mika commanded. "Leave him with his grief. He will one day beg for the relief of death."

Ken walked up to Mika who still held the bloodied knife. She smiled and performed a quasi ceremonial pose as she presented Ken with the knife.

"I do believe you wanted this."

Ken accepted the blade. It was made of black iron and had a rubber handle. The blade itself was jagged toothed, curved and two inches long. It was not fancy, it was actually rather crude.

Mika gleefully grabbed Ken hands and headed for the church's exit. Sam crawled to Florence deceased body. He howled out in pain and horror, and as he cried Mika turned and smiled saying only. "Smooches..."

"You didn't have to kill her," Ken said.

Mika turned to him smiling, "Of course I didn't. But you got to admit, it made things interesting."

Fulton Street was busy and Mika's cheer echoed through the grim block. Her glee shimmered off her smooth lifeless skin.

"I *didn't have* to save you," Mika reminded her pupil. "But I did. So stop with the incessant bitching."

Mika was getting tired of Ken complaining that never seemed to end. The Mortal Coil; even after one is removed from it has some lingering human emotions remaining.

"Where are we going?" Ken asked.

"To see some friends," Mika said, removing the the small phone out of her pocket.

Mika knew one thing was certain; those three boys all knew each other *very* well. No one sets out to murder someone without having a deep trust of their partners. Murder is a very intimate art. Chances are they have contacted each other.

Mika attempted to use Sam's iPhone but struggled to understand the phone. Her fingers wildly traversed across the smooth glass screen."

"I loathe technology," she confessed. "Can you make this thing work?"

After a smooth strokes Ken revealed the texts messages Mika knew was there already.

"Joshua and Mark Montgomery," Ken said. "Found there FaceBook account."

"See that's why I deleted mine," Mika joked. "I hate the technology of this time. It's not innovative, it's just... just..."

The vampire pondered the most effective word; when she found it she snapped her fingers. "Invasive. No privacy. You never know when your sucking on the neck of a toddler's nanny if the webcam is recording you. Last thing we need is a vampire attack uploaded online."

"How many of *us* are there?"

Mika shrugged her shoulders, laying her thin frame against the adjacent building. "Not many, perhaps, one hundred thousand, most likely less than that."

Ken was shocked by the low number of vampires. Yesterday vampires were a legend and stories on film. Tonight they were his brethren, his race.

"Why so few? "

"Vampires don't get along very well," Mika wanted to know where those boys were. "Where are we heading."

"They both work at *Sunny Suds Laundry.*"

Josh and Mark were tweaking out. The two brothers had made a decent amount of meth, so tasting some of the product was expected.

The Brooklyn Laundromat was a front for the brother meth lab. So while locals were scrubbing out their underwear; the two brothers were cooking up crystal.

Josh as known as RedRangerRyan was lighting up. Getting high was the only thing that calmed his nerves. And after what happened yesterday, calm nerves seemed to be a thing of the past.

Everything about that job went wrong, everything. Josh couldnot sleep at all that night and it was not just because of his meth binge. He kept seeing Ken's face in his nightmares.

Mark handled the murder a lot better. Far as he was concerned all he did was beat someone up. It was Sam who took it to the next level. And if any police were to confront him about it he and his brother would simply blame Sam.

Simple enough plan.

Mark kept his mind on cooking; with as much meth he smokes plus the buyer, he had a *long* night ahead of him. Or an extremely *abbreviated* night; especially since two vampires were stalking the small rundown commercial property looking to settle the score.

"Now try to control yourself," Mika said to Ken. "I understand the hunger can take control of you. But you must remain in control."

"How?"

"It's like sex," Mika answered vulgarly. "Just when it starts to get too good, I mean so good you can't stand it: you slow down and take a second to recover. Bask the beauty of it. Then go in again."

"I want Josh," Ken declared. "He's the reason all this is happening."

"You should thank him. Thanks to him you were made immortal. And I'm not hungry. I'm here only for moral support. This is all you."

Ken ripped off his bloodied top; his soft pale skin was jagged with muscles. He slipped his right hand in his pocket and removed the small pocket knife and crept through the front door.

The golden bell rang softly which pulled Mark from cooking. At these hours it was most likely a customer and they had no interest in washing clothes. Mark grabbed a few small bags of meth and headed to the front.

Mark was met by a shirtless Ken; before Mark could react Ken threw the small blade at Mark's head, piercing his brain. Before Mark's body hit the ground Ken caught him then quickly sank his fangs in his throat.

Aroused, Ken held Mark drinking from his neck. Taking Mika's advice Ken restrained himself. Ken could feel Mark's body go limp. As he slurped messily at the wound Ken dove deeper and deeper into ecstasy.

But then something happened. The blood begin to turn sour slowly; Ken could taste the bile rise into the bloodstream. Ken broke away.

Ken removed the blade from Mark's brain. A small smile tickled at Ken's fanged mouth. With the pocket knife Ken viciously slashed at Mark's face.

Ken was distracted by his vampiric nature. He had gave into his gruesomely evil temperament. Then he stopped; he heard a lighter spark, from the way it sound he could tell it was in another room.

Ken walked lightly to the backroom lit only by black lights where the brothers cooked their meth. Ken drug the blade across the washer as he followed his instincts.

Josh could not make out who was standing before him. But he could tell by the body it was not his brother. Whoever it was, the person was holding knife.

"Ryan, dude is that you?" Josh asked coughing from meth smoke.

"So that's where you got 'Ryan' from," Ken said. "One day I'm going to have to meet 'Ryan'. He's the only person missing from this little story."

Josh placed his glass pipe down. He tried to focus his eyes but his pupil could not process what was before him.

"Dude, if you want some money," Josh said trying to deescalate the situation, "all the money we have made is in that washer under the clothes."

"I'm not here for money," Ken said. Ken then pointed the blade in an intimidating manner. "I'm here for you."

"It's you isn't it?" Josh said. "This isn't a dream, I'm not fucking *tweaking* out am I?"

"No, you're definitely *tweaking* out," Ken clarified. "But it's me. Would you like a closer look?"

Using his blurring vampire speed, Ken nose met Josh's. Ken's eye began to glow a dark honey color and his fangs were exposed.

This is Death, Josh thought.

"Oh my God, I'm so sorry," Josh cried out.

"Don't be sorry," Ken said smiling, "I'm so thankful for you. If it wasn't for your sociopathic, fag bashin', hate crime; I wouldn't be made into what I am now. So let me show you my appreciation."

Ken grabbed Josh by his shirt dragging him into his bite. Josh screamed out as the vampire angrily fed off his blood. Josh went into cardiac arrest and the vampire still drained him.

Josh was on his back, Ken pinned him in place to the floorboards. Ken pulled away from the chocking Josh. The ruby blood drops coated Ken's mouth as he watched the sickly yellow Josh coughed on his own blood.

Ken's eyes remain locked with Josh's. Josh wanted to stare Ken down; he wanted to see what killed him. He wanted to understand it, even if only seconds before death.

Josh coughs began to slow down and were replaced by gasps. Josh slowly died as Ken stared at him. Josh made one more hoarse gasp before death took him.

"Thank you," Ken said before unpinning him.

Silence befell. They were all dead; all those who conspired to murder him. But the void within him was not filled. Something was still missing.

"You still feel it don't you?" Mika asked as she slithered behind him. "You thought that killing them would make you *feel* – anything."

"It just made me more confused," Ken confessed.

"Well allow me to clear things up for you," Mika said. "You are officially a vampire. Before you fed on human's, before you abandoned your humanity, your life could have been saved.

"You could have lived in the sunlight; you could have had a mortal existence. But now you have nothing to look forward to but infinite nights and death. Accept your loneliness and fate and make something of your existence."

Mika smiled and began to turn leave but Ken, now even more confused stopped her. Grabbing her arm Ken demanded to know what she was doing. What did she mean by loneliness? Why would he be alone? He demanded answers.

"We are demons; we live for the destruction of man. But some of us, the real innovative demons like to watch you mortals destroy each other.

"Before you drank from Josh, ultimately killing him, you were still mortal. It pleased me watching a hybrid, but still a mortal killing his own. Just as I made Sam kill Flo."

Mika then used her enormous strength to throw Ken many feet across the room. His face colliding against the black light and tore into his flesh.

"But you're my-savior, you're all I have now," Ken protested.

Mika giggled girlishly. "Kid, do I really look like, a *savior*?" She let out another giggle at Ken's dismay. "Don't look so blue –at least you're immortal."

And with a dark curtsy Mika walked out of the room leaving her pupil to live in this world alone. *In the darkness.*

Chapter

3

Aryk

Rosewood, Florida 2012

I am the embodiment of evolution; a Dead Thing. I am a vampire, which is quite the fascinating creature to be. Today, tales of effeminate, castrated, powdered face she-boys litter bookstores and dance around the fantasies of teenage girls everywhere. In the age of vampiric mass-consumption, the reveal of vampires should have already happened, right? Wrong.

Gotta love mortal ignorance. The only thing that matches human ignorance is their lack of a moral compass.

Every night I deliver death to those who crave it. I find immortality more bearable when not killing the most innocent mortals I can find. Earth has over six billion people, weeding out the one's yearning death is pretty simple.

Before a vampire had to lurk the streets at night looking for a victim, someone usually alone, someone who would not be missed; the forgotten. Today social media networks help locate people who are desperate and suicidal. Consider me the undead doctor Kevorkian; bringing the mercy of death to those who wants it.

But all Immortals are not made the same. Dead Things are not all the same.

Dead Things aren't all the same. As like humans, some vampires pose powers that others do not have. In the case of, Aryk Isaac Killen, his powers are one of the most formidable and deadly.

A dark figure cut across the ink Floridian midnight sky. The moon shone brightly in the darkness as the ominous figure loomed ever closer to his destination. He slowly flutters to the ground, his long coat waving like the cape of The Dark Knight.

Aryk's black leather boots landed silently on the dewy grass. He had two hours before daybreak. Cecil's blood was not as satisfying as he thought it would be. Aryk walked into the dark forest, he pondered what to do about the situation. He could slip to Cedar Key and pick up some "fast food," but decided against it.

Most older vampires like Aryk, preferred to be away from the masses when they rest. Aryk understood that humans are unpredictable and a vampire could never be too comfortable living among mortals.

Aryk walked deeper into the forest; one hundred years ago this town flourished with people, mostly black. Rosewood, Florida was burned to the ground when a white woman from the neighboring town of Sumner accused a black man of rape. The false accusation caused hundreds of drunken white men to invade Rosewood killing all those who lived there. Only a few escaped with their lives.

The ghost town had been abandoned ever since. Rosewood was not only forgotten by the world but also by history. Aryk found solace in this cemetery; he thought the idea of a vampire living in a ghost town was very appropriate.

Hidden deep in the forest of Rosewood, was Aryk's lair. Aryk's house from the outside looked like a vine-covered, rundown victorian mansion. The inside was a very modern, sheik, southern palace with bone white marble floors.

"Where you been at," Angelique asked Aryk as he walked through the door.

"California," Aryk said as he kicked off his boots. Aryk always loved the lovely state of California. It was his favorite state in all the Americas – Aryk always could smell the sunlight on the skin of his victims. The sun – all Dead Things miss the glow of the sun.

"Hate California," Angelique said was she picked up Aryk's boots. "All the nuts and fruits roll right in California."

Angelique was mortal, female, and forty one years old. She stood five feet and five inches, one hundred and twenty pounds, ebony skin with long black tresses. Angelique lived with Aryk in his home her entire life. Aryk and Angelique's connection was through blood. Angelique was Aryk's last living family member.

Over the years Aryk grew very lonely; he missed his mortality, his family, his roots. In 1947 he found his cousin Minnie Earl, a young creole girl from

Florida; she was Aryk's fifth cousin on his mother's side. Aryk took care of Minnie Earl who would go on to bare one child, Angelique.

Minnie purpose was to take care of Aryk as he rested during the day. During the day Dead Things are at their most venerable. Historically, wild mobs would hunt out vampires, burning them as they slept. So wise Dead Things often employed humans to protect them as they slept.

Minnie, not having any mortal family, took to Aryk her immortal cousin and showered him with love and loyalty. Though unsure at first through Minnie Aryk rekindled that remaining trace of humanity that still flickered inside of him.

Angelique brash personality was a contrast to her mother's subservient attitude. Angelique, raised in the new world of women's and African American rights, rejected the idea of being nothing more than a maid. Aryk appreciated her independence, and hope that she would bear a child like her mother before her. But now in her early forty's it appears to be unlikely.

"Kill anything interesting?" Angelique asked. Angelique enjoyed hearing about the villains Aryk would kill. Aryk only dined on murders, rapist, child molesters, and other human fiends. But Aryk also killed the innocent, innocents like Cecil. Aryk often times withheld those victims from Angelique fearing that she could not handle the truth. The truth was Aryk was a killer – and Angelique was still a mortal. Loyalty would be to her true brethren.

"I went to the beach," Aryk answered. His voice was short, he really didn't want to tell her any details. Angelique could sense the agitation in the vampire's voice, but her curiosity made her hunger for more details. "Sunrise will be soon. I'll see you tonight."

"You never have time," Angelique complained.

"All I have... is time."

This isn't over, Angelique thought. Aryk was hiding something, but that wasn't new. She suspected he hid many things from her. But whatever his secrets were she had every intentions from prying them from her undead cousin.

Aryk walked into his bedroom; quite a magnificent bedroom. Aryk, a vampire with lots of disposable income, had spent his money on decorating his home. Aryk's bedroom had fancy portraits, plush throw rugs, and a large California king to accent his earth-tone colored room.

Immortality, it sounds really nice on paper, but Aryk had begun to experience the reverb of living forever. Living everyday doing the same monotonous shit makes forever is a long time. Aryk had killed many times and most of them were very anticlimactic. Humans are mostly virgins to death; only a few of them ever come back from it. The average human lays there and screams. Dead fish.

Aryk needed something to stimulate his vampiric urges, and killing humans just was not stimulating anymore. They do not taste as good anymore; all those preservatives and medication they ingest really eroded their blood. Vampires cannot even get a decent drink anymore.

Aryk scanned himself through the large mirror in his bedroom. He could still see the ruby hue on his lips from feeding off Cecil. This is what he was – this was *all* he was. Soullessness, sullen, alone.

Aryk had been alone for years, though Angelique was not his only "friend," Aryk had no vampire partner in decades. Aryk himself had never procreated either. Creating another vampire is a sacred event in the vampire world, one that Aryk did not take lightly.

Still, Aryk yearned for some connection. His only connection to the living world was Angelique. And she was a pariah in mortal standards. Over a lifetime of eternal night; the depression related with vampirism had set in. overwhelmed by his vampiric rage that vampire angrily shattered his mirror with a punch. His fist penetrated the plastered wall – he removes it from the crater exposing a slightly red and dusted fist. He reached quickly for a shard and sliced wildly across his cherubic face.

Blood splattered against the wall – the vampires Powers had taken effect and the healing process was almost completed. Aryk was getting frustrated with his immortality; he forgot what it was like to feel. It had been like this over one-hundred and Seventy-five years.

I'm indestructible.

Aryk walked over to his large cherry wood dresser and retrieved a small box. In it was a small photograph dated 1899. The photo had begun to curl at edges due to time. The young girl smiled innocently – but her confidence was apparent in her eyes. Her crimson curls and jade colored eyes appeared only gray in the photo. The vampire held the photo close his face and inhaled the sweet memories of Scarlett. Aryk stripped nude and climbed into bed.

Los Angeles, California
Early August 2012

Scott had just walked home after a brief run on the beach. He had returned home from Iraq where Scott was a Marine since 2004. He was twenty seven, six feet and one inch, athletic and build strong. Scott used his fitness routine as a distraction from the stress he was experiencing. Scott had Post-Traumatic Stress from his time in Iraq, he would often have flashes and he would be right back in Baghdad. The night terros happen often, leaving his bed often wet with urine and sweat.

Scott arrived home from his morning jog when he noticed two Los Angeles Police Squad cars parked outside of his parents home. *Damn,* he thought, *they are serious about those photo radar things.* Scott was confident he had been snapped a few time for his reckless driving. It was time to face the music.

Scott walked inside of the Brentwood estate and was greeted by his crying mother. "It's Cecil."

His mother could not verbalize anything else. The reality had yet to even reach her, she could not even begin to explain it to Scott.

"Mom, what's going on?" Scott asked; his mother remained mute. "Mom, what's wrong with Cecil.

"Cecil!" Scott called out to his sister as if she was in the room upstairs. Scott was confident that this had to be about drugs or skipping curfew. There was no way this could be serious.

One of the officers finally spoke up, "You're sister was found under the Santa Monica Pier. Her wrists had been slashed; it's being investigated but it's likely a suicide."

"No..." Scott said skeptically. "There's a mistake, it's gotta be."

"Her identification was found on her body," The officer stated rather matter-of-factly.

Scott had seen many friends die, some right in front of him while in war. But the death of Cecil, a beautiful young girl with her whole life ahead of her devastated him. Very few things sustained the already fractured soul of Scott Jason Wellington, and losing his sister was another crashing blow.

Scott had not learned to process grief, even with therapy he had yet to learn how to maintain his emotions. Scott walked upstairs silently as his tearful mother called after him. Scott did not have the emotional stability to help her; she was on her own.

Scott walked into his sister's room; her walls were covered with pictures of Justin Beiber, something that her emotionally-anorexic friends would be shock to see. Scott climbed in his sister's full-size bed and pulled her pink blankets over himself.

Scott lost it all. Scott laid there alone and cried to himself noiselessly. As he cried Scott sniffed her comforter trying to smell Cecil. He wanted to bring her back to life if only for a second. He could smell her vanilla body spray, he could hear her sharp as daggers wit, and for one moment, Cecil was resurrected.

Chapter

4

Scott hated hospitals; his father died in one, this exact hospital, Cedar-Sinai. Scott went with his mother to identify the body. Scott waited until noon before he could leave the house.

The morgue has a smell, he could smell the agents that were used to clean and disinfect the instruments. He could smell ethanol. He could smell death. *Is this all people have to look forward to?* Scott thought to himself.

"I still think you should wait until the funeral Scott," Scott's mother, Marcie said.

"I'm already here," Scott said. He was not going anywhere until he saw her body.

Scott and his mother were brought into the morgue where a gurney sat in the middle of the room with a body covered with a sheet. He knew it was her, he knew she was dead but the reality hit him when the sheet was pulled back to show her bruised face. Her cheeks were plump and purple. It did not look like

Cecil, but it was. Scott could see the dried blood in Cecil's nose.

"My baby," Marcie said as she cried to herself.

Mortals always know that death is coming for them. Death and taxes are always promised in the mortal coilbut when death comes sooner than anticipated, then and only then, is it considered a tragedy.

Scott returned to the lobby where he sat silently and thought to himself. It was just him and his mother now. He had never been so alone. Scott accepted role as the "man of the house" when his father died when he was only seventeen. The family processed the tragedy and moved forward. But neither Scott nor Marcie had it in them to face yet another tragedy.

Left alone with his thought, Scott sunk further in depression .Scott could feel hand grab his, it was small and feminine.

"I'm sorry, honey," Beth said. Beth was Scott's girlfriend, the two had such an intense emotional bond only she could bring him to baseline. Beth sat next to Scott, who put his head on her lap and began to sob. Beth took her left hand and began to stroke his hair. She loving massaged the back of his head, running her fingers ever so gently through his curly chestnut hair.

Beth had supported Scott emotionally since he returned from Iraq. They had dated since college and she had only wanted him to ask her the question that all girls want to hear. Scott could not give himself emotionally to anyone, but if he could it would be with Beth.

Beth was five feet and six inches, soft lily blonde hair, small but effective frame, and full soft pink lips. Her beauty was impressive, even by Los Angeles standards. Her heart was as beautiful as she was and Scott would need to rely on the love she had for him to sustain himself.

"Let's get some lunch," Beth suggested.

"I can't leave her," Scott replied.

"You're mom is ready to go," Beth said.

"I can't leave Cecil," Scott said.

"You won't, you can never leave her ever," Beth said. "She's apart of you, so you will always have her in your heart." She pulled him in close for a soft kiss, the fire of her mouth melted the glacier over Scott's heart. "But we need to go – she would want you go."

Beth watched Scott fork aimlessly at his manicotti. Scott has always been known for his insatiable appetite and watching him avoid his favorite dish was concerning. She could see his sister was fresh on his mind and wanted to change the topic.

"Let's go to Florida," Beth declared.

"I don't think a trip is what I need," Scott said. "We have to plan for Cecil's funeral."

"I understand," Beth said meekly. But she could not just back down, she had to get Scott out of this rut. "My team found something in Tasmania a few years back, this tribal urn. The locals believe it is connected to the Thylacine."

Breaking the silence that both Scott and his mother shared because they were not at all sure what Beth was talking about Scott asked, "The who?"

"Thylacine, the Tasmania Tiger, or wolf, depending on which text you read," Beth said. "But the locals called it Tassie. It was a Tiger with a wolf head that stalked the livestock in Tasmania."

"Folklore?" Marcie asked.

"No, it was a real animal," Beth clarified. "However it was a marsupial, if you were to see it you would think it was a dog or something. The native people of Tasmania had a high respect for the animal. The European settlers however, no so much; they blamed the animal for killing cattle and sheep. So they were hunted until extinction."

"Nice..." Scott said with a hint of sarcasm. "What does this have to do with Florida?"

"*Well* a Floridian Museum would like to showcase the piece," Beth announced. "It's my first find to be displayed in a museum."

"That's excellent Beth," Marcie said.

Scott reached over and grabbed her hand and gave her his first smile of the day, "Proud of you Mary-Beth."

"My boss has a home down there, he wanted me to check out some of his findings – it could be interesting."

"Is it by Miami?" Scott asked, hoping to switch up the Californian sun for the Floridian sub-tropical sky.

"No, not really."

Curious to know of any other reason to visit Florida except to go Miami, Scott interrogated, "Then where are we going – you know I hate snakes."

Resisting the urge to roll her eyes Beth sweetly responded, "There won't be any snakes, we're just visiting a friend for a few minutes. It's going to be good for you, you get a nice southern style meal and you can commune with nature."

"I think it's a great idea," Marci supported. She wanted to be able to grieve without her emotionally fragile son see her break down. She placed a compassionate hand on Scott shoulder, mother and son caught each other's eyes. Without saying any more Marci told her son all he needed to know – he *needed* to go for both of them.

Sumner, Florida

Angelique was never one to mince words, so she meant ever word when she told the butcher, "Bitch, if you don't find my motherfucking pigs blood, it's gonna be me and you."

Angelique ordered this blood days ago; it was promised to be there. She needed the blood for the last ingredient to her spell. Angelique had tampered with the dark arts for many years and being affiliated with a vampire always helps. Aryk often had access to text that were rare and very potent.

Angelique needed the blood for an offering; she needed help with fertility, so why not invoke the tribal Goddess Athena to help with that. In the world of man nothing is free, and it is the same in the world of magic.

"Look lady, we don't have it," the man said, agitated with Angelique entire presence. "So you need to leave right now."

"Are you telling me you don't have my blood?"

"No, lady. Beat it!"

"You're gonna wish you did," Angelique said in a warning tone. Mutely she cursed, *In the name of Kahlil, father of vengeance, take away his manhood.* She planted a quick curse that causes impotence – one of the first enchantments she learned.

Angelique returned home to Rosewood, which in itself is not an easy task. This is mainly because the roads are not very automobile friendly. Most roads that did exist are covered in bush and greenery. Due to this, Angelique parks the 2012 Nissan Maxima, dipped a deep crimson candy paint, in the forest and walks one mile to the house. Aryk loved his car, but he rarely drove. Like many things in Aryk's world it was merely for decoration.

The sun had almost set and Aryk was already awake. Aryk was in the restroom, a room he uses only for showers since vampires do not have a digestive system nor do they use the toilet.

Aryk was fresh out the shower brushing his long wavy black hair. His hair was his pride and joy; even as a mortal. He always said you can tell how someone is feeling by their hair. He had never seen hair so beautiful before and after almost two hundred years; he has still not seen any that could compare.

"It's just hair," Angelique said as she spied on him from the hall.

"A vampire's hair never changes, even if you cut it, dye it, it doesn't matter. It will eventually, and often times rather rapidly, return to the state it was in before the vampire had turn immortal."

"What's the problem?"

"I've gotten a gray streak in the back of my head," Aryk said as he held up the iron strand.

"Nigga, are you serious?"

Aryk turned around to face Angelique; his eyes intense and his fangs exposed, "I do *NOT* like that word."

"My mistake," Angelique said apologetically. "But *still* are you serious?"

"Vampires only change when there is a significant change," Aryk said. "I last felt like this when Aria was killed."

"What happen then?'

"I went gray – all of it. I will consult Luke; he is the eldest vampire I know."

"He's in LA, and sundown there isn't for another three hours," Angelique said. "Maybe I could find something in the text..."

"I must depart," Aryk declared. "I will see you in the morning."

And with barely any words Aryk walked down the stairs, however Angelique wouldn't just allow him to drop such a bomb and say no more. "How did it go back –you're hair?"

"I fed –a lot."

Los Angeles, California

He had to go where it happened. Scott hoped he would reach some level of closure if goes to the last place Cecil lived. Scott stood under the Santa Monica Pier; yellow police tape was still webbed across the wooden beams.

"So this is where it happened," Scott pondered to himself tearfully. Scott chased closure but it was tied to the tail of a dragon. Scott could not accept that his sister slit her wrist under the Santa Monica Pier. She hated Santa Monica – she always said that all the stuck up skanks lived there.

Why here, he thought. Nothing was adding up. The police stated that she wrote a suicide letter also, however it didn't read like anything he had ever seen her write. But it was her handwriting – down to the smiley face that she used after signing her name.

Today is the day,

Today is the day where I say goodbye. Mom I love you. I love you so much that I couldn't do this at the house. You've been through enough. I love you, Scott, and my friends but... I just can't anymore.

Scott held the letter to his nose and took a sniff – he couldn't smell Cecil's boyish cologne that she sprayed on all her letters. *She didn't write this*, Scott thought. Any note she ever left was covered in *Big Pony 1* by Ralph Lauren. Cecil did not write this letter.

Across the town in Compton Aryk had just made it to Los Angeles. Not all vampires can fly, but Aryk was very efficient with it. Compton was legendary for its violence and gang relation. One of Los Angeles most notorious hamlets, but it was also the home for a very old vampire named, Luke.

Aryk walked up Irvine, a heavily drug infested street in Compton. Aryk stuck out like a sore thumb. He was shirtless with a dark blazer, dark tight denim slacks, and top hat. He particularly caught the attention of a bunch of young hoodlums who saw it as an opportunity to hassle him.

"Damn, man," one of the four young men said. "Is it a full moon or something, cause all the damn freaks are coming out tonight."

"Nigga it ain't Halloween," another young man said with a blue bandanna wrap around his wrist.

"Why you up in this bitch looking like a faggot Abe Lincoln."

"I'm looking for Luke," Aryk answered monotone and flat.

"Uh, it looks like you wanna make a deposit," the first young man said. "I'm Cedric, and you can make your deposits to Cedric *Trust*. And *trust* me, nigga; you gonna wanna make that shit A-sap or imma have to murk yo ass."

Aryk let a small smile grace his face, with lightening speed he reached and grabbed Cedric by his throat lifting him two feet off the ground. Cedric was grabbed so fast he had no time to even process what had happened to him. His crew reached for their pistols but was stopped by the vampire's words.

"I will crush his wind pipe like a grape before you can shoot one bullet," Aryk warned. Aryk exposes his fangs and Cedric's eyes dilated from the fear; he knew he was going to die. "So Cedric, consider this me giving back to *the community*, by letting your friends get a pass. Next time, I won't be so pleasant." Aryk released his grip and allowed Cedric to fall on his bottom.

Cedric friends dispersed and Cedric sat there on the ground, eyes locked with Aryk. He was stuck like a deer in headlights until Aryk said, "Run along now," then Aryk roared like a wild cat and Cedric got to his feet and ran off, boxer exposed due to his sagging.

"Kids..." Aryk said with a small chuckle.

"You're good at scaring people," Luke said.

Luke was the closest to an Ancient walking around today. Luke was four hundred and thirty nine years old. Most vampires once they reach five hundred tend to experience psychosis and what human's often get in their later years: senility.

Luke was originally from Ghana, he was the leader of his tribe, and when he was turned he even lead his maker. Luke is also known for his knowledge and horrifying strength. His physical appearance is thirty two years old, but his once brown eyes have began to fade hazel, a result of vampiric aging.

"You're dressed like them," Aryk said as he checked out Luke's Kangol tracksuit and fitted LA Dodgers baseball cap. "Except you still look dated."

"Fashion changes too often for me," Luke teased. Luke had mastered the American accent, finding it opens more doors. "One minute its Tupac the next it's Soulja Boy."

"Now it's Drake."

Luke sucked his teeth in disgust, "I prefer Tupac."

Aryk walked into Luke modest two bedrooms house. It looked like a mortal's home, a broke mortal.

"For a very old and powerful creature," Aryk said as he scanned his home. "you live in a very meager home."

"Am I not glamorous enough for you, Mr. Killen?"

"Actually, no."

"Aren't you getting too old for all those distractions you have in your life," Luke countered. "One can only stay with the joneses so long – trust me I've tried. But ten mortal years is like a week to me now."

"I'm not even two hundred," Aryk retorted. "But I know the feeling."

Aryk was beginning to feel the effects of eternal life. As mortals age, time appears to moves quicker because they become more accustomed to the ever moving clock. For Dead Things it's the same – only difference is they tend to outlive the average human life expectancy.

"I feel fine," Aryk lied."Well tell that to that gray-ass hair on top of your head."

Aryk immediately touched his hair, and then it dawned on him. "Reading my thoughts? How rude."

"Vampires only change once every two hundred and fifty years; you're changing because something enormous is coming; something effulgent."

"'Devastating enormous' or *'Precious enormous'?*"

Luke closed his eyes and tapped into the universe. The Universe has all the answers to all questions. But The Universe has never been known for its directness, but surely its precision. Powerful being like Luke can tap into The Universe's central nervous system and force these answers out.

"I can't tell you," Luke said.

"Why-the-hell not?"

"Because The Universe is going to reveal it to you, soon."

Aryk put his hand on his hip with disappointment, "'*soon'* to a vampire could be years."

"This won't be years," Luke said, eyes still closed. "We are talking days. Assuming it hasn't happen already."

Sumner, Florida

"OH FUCK!" Sam cried as he dropped the urn.

"What did you do?" Vanna asked.

"I just dropped this god damned jar," Sam complained. He roughly racked his scalp with his finger nails. The pressure was starting to take a toll on the aging archeologist.

It was his last dig. Sam now aged fifty nine, had grown sick of travel all across the globe to dig on often time fruitless missions. Six months ago it was Tasmania; and it was the same. He came, he dug, and he found nothing. Well, almost nothing. While in the pit in a eucalyptus forest in south Tasmania, Sam discovered a small jar. The jar itself looked like any tribal, clay jar, Holocenic in date, and surprising sturdy.

When the jar fell it remained intake, except the top on the jar was loosened and fell off. With the top opened, dust and other particles fell out of the jar. Sam, still an archeologist at heart grabbed his magnifying glass to get a closer look. Along with a lot of indistinguishable particles, bone was an obvious component.

Then he heard it. A wheezing, scratchy, bark. Sam looked to his right and there it stood; thinned frame, dog-like animal. But it was no dog. Its face was that similar to a hyena. Without a chance to defend himself, the animal darted towards Sam.

Sam got to his feet as quickly as he could but was tackled to the ground by the creature. Pinned to the ground, the animal looked down to Sam. The animal's eyes looked dark and empty, feral and evil. Sam cried out for his wife, Vanna as the animal began to open his mouth.

Its mouth – it's frightening mouth open more and more as if it had no limits to how wide it could become. Gargantuan fangs exposed, mouth open one hundred twenty degrees, Sam could only let out one more scream before the stripped-back dog demon ate his face.

Vanna darted back into the home after hearing her husband's screams. When Vanna reached the study she saw a nude, small child, dark ebony skinned boy with long smooth hair. He desperately fed on the remains of her husband. The child looked up at Vanna, with blood and chunks of flesh hanging from his mouth.

And with a dark grin the child pounced Vanna, knocking her to the ground. Vanna was shocked by how fast and strong the small child was. Pinned by the boy to the ground and Vanna too was devoured by the child.

The plague was released.

Chapter

5

What you gotta understand is: it is in the bite. The Bite is something that has mystified scientist, magician, priest, and all those people who freight over such things. In fact, The Bite has a simpler break down than most people know. Simply put, The Bite affects you in two ways: physical and metaphysical.

Physically The Bite carries a toxin; the toxins attack the central nervous system causing a very mild paralysis. If a vampire's unnatural strength did not hold its prey in place, the toxins would usually do the trick. It takes a truly remarkable human to escape a vampire assault, let alone its bite. Those strong enough to tear away usually lose a piece of their throat.

Vampires love the classics; so the clichéd "carotid-artery-bite" is usually employed. Though technically it is the most unsophisticated way of feeding; it is the preferred technique. It requires more sucking however it is usually the most exposed artery on the human body and thus the easiest to get to.

The Bite usually takes the human by surprise; most of them are more shocked that someone is trying to bite them. The Bite usually takes all the adrenaline out of the human. With all the fight taken out of the mortal, they simply succumb to the vampires attack.

But as horrible as that is; it is the metaphysical effects of The Bite that gets you. Yes, the most dangerous aspects are the most hidden. Assuming one could escape the vampire's bite, throat intake; it does not mean the human is free of the vampire.

The Bite tends to leave a long term hypnotic effect on the mortal. If a human somehow survives; the vampire will have a long term influence over him or her. I cannot really describe exactly how that works.

Cannot give away *all* of the surprises. But *The Blood* makes The Bite look like nothing. Once The Blood gets involved you enter a whole new territory. But let's not get ahead of ourselves.

The Bite, like all things related to dead things, is subjective. The Bite on one vampire is not the same as another. Depending on age and pedigree The Bite could have more or less effects. Aryk's bite is one of the most dangerous in the modern world.

By 2011, Aryk may have killed well over eighty thousand humans. He has killed mothers, husbands, brothers, sisters, women, men, and babies. A vampire of his age had a bit of a reputation for his ruthlessness.

It was only recently that Aryk started paying attention to who he was killing. For the first one hundred years of all vampires' life; they live only in the blind rave of blood and destruction. But Aryk, who is almost two hundred, had become quite bored with the rigmarole that was vampirism.

Aryk became excited only when he killed someone who wanted to die. The subliminally suicidal were one of his favorite foods, second only to those who hunt him. When humans hunt for death in this fashion, Aryk cannot help but help speed up the process.

Los Angles, California

Scott had for weeks now hunted for his sister's killer. Cecil was killed on the Santa Monica Pier. Due to their family name and status, many private investigators along with police had been investigating the case. Scott had just returned home from Iraq to hear that his sister was murdered.

Cecil's body was found on the shore; her wrists were slashed along with a suicide letter found in her purse near a camp site not too far from the body. Cecil had a history of depression and even suicide attempts. The police officers had just closed the case and ruled it a suicide.

Scott did not want to accept that it was a suicide. Scott refused to accept Cecil's death because it went against anything he felt. His gut kept him alive in Fallujah. As long as he denied her death, Cecil still existed. He could not let her go, not until he could make sense of her death.

His reasoning was simple; for her to have killed herself, she would have slit her own wrist; both wrist. Secondly, if Cecil wanted to kill herself: why not just overdose on the numerous prescription medications she had at her disposal. Why in such a public fashion? It was wrong, all wrong according to Scott.

Scott was only twenty seven and his younger sister was already dead. Her death was a blow that was harder than he could handle. The little girl that he protected, cherished, loved had been ripped out of this world too soon.

Scott, already suffering from Post Traumatic Syndrome from the Iraq War of 2000's had no one to talk about the trauma. His mother had learned the art of ignoring reality so the family never talked about the possibility of Cecil being murdered. After returning to the states to find his friends had all started family and left; Scott was forced to face the world alone. So Scott turned to Jim Bean.

Scott sat inside of *Phish Head*, a Santa Monica bar located not too far from the beach. It was 9:36pm and Scott was already drunk. Scott's brown eyes peered deep inside his half way empty Jack and Water.

Scott's body was chiseled out of stone and his face was rough with stubbly moss-like brown hairs. Scott had not slept much in the past weeks and his distress was very apparent. The scruffy bad boy look usually gets the eye of the female population.

"You've been looking at the drink for a long time," an attractive female bar patron said. "Can I get you something else?"

Scott, always a fan of lovely face, smiles. But more than getting laid, Scott wanted to wallow in his own despair.

"I'm alright," Scott said politely. "I'm just looking for a nice solitaire night."

"Girlfriend?"

"No," he lied.

"*I'm* Shelly," she said with a seductive smile. Shelly's body was tight and smooth, and her short mocha dressed melted down her ample frame. Tan, pink lips, MAC makeup.

"*I'm* not interested," Scott said, mildly agitated.

Shelly not one for rejection was a little thrown by Scott's response. She wouldn't just settle for that answer. With a smile she replied, "Of course you are. Let's get you another round." She gestured for the barkeep to give them refills.

"You are really persisitent, I'll give you that," Scott sail with a smile impressed by Shelly's ballsy attitude. They shared a smile and proceeded to toast. "What are we toasting to?"

"Meeting new friends," Shelly shot back and smile and clinked the two glasses together. She was taken aback by the potency of the drink – but her slightly tomboy spirit wouldn't allow her shock to reach her face.

"What are you doing here, by yourself," Scott asked after downing his drink. "Far too pretty to be trying to pick my drunk ass up."

"You're right." She finished her drink and shot back a flirtatious smirk. The smile was all that was needed to stimulate Scott. Even drunk Scott didn't want to possibly sully his relationship with Beth – she was all he had now.

"I really need to get out of here," he declared.

"Well, I won't hold you up," she said before walking away. *Gay*, she thought.

Aryk watched from a far. Scott had returned to the site where Cecil was killed on numerous occasions. This did not happen without getting Aryk's attention; after all, Cecil had been a victim of his.

The human sparked the vampires attention, initially Scott feared that he was *cacciatore di vampiri* – humans specifically trained to kill vampires. His militant like posture is what put the idea in his mind.

But much to his immense amusement he discovered that Scott was actually Cecil's brother.

*I **have** to get points if I kill the brother, too,* Aryk thought. The sociopath in Aryk made this next kill all the more... insatiable. A new game began.

By 10:16 pm Scott had left the bar, he went to a nearby alley where he took a much needed leak. Scott noticed a man rummaging through trash, the man was homeless, and was talking to himself.

"That bitch... The cunt..." the man said as he dug through the dumpster.

The man was clearly insane, trapped in the Wonderful World of Disney. However the the magic of fire water started playing with Scott's mind.

Insane, misogynistic; this was just the type of guy that *could* have killed Cecil. He was the poster boy for psycho-killers; he even had the schizophrenic rambling to himself going on. He was the type of man, based solely on ignorance Scott thought that could have killed his sister on a beach that was barely a mile away.

Murderer, Scott thought. His mind raced. The alcohol was the cause; he began to see the blood the

Cecil was covered in. He could see the fear in her eyes; a fear he knew all too well. Scott could see the bodies that he piled up in Iraq; the men that Scott killed while in war. And then that word again.

Murderer.

Murderer,   *murderer,*   *murderer...* "Murderer!!!" Scott screamed.

Scott stormed, drunkenly, towards the startled bum. "Was it you, huh, did you do it?" Scott quizzed as he grabbed the man by his tattered and oily denim jacket. The man, so afraid, cried frantically and ranted in a word-salad. The incoherent rant was peppered with "um's" and "pleases".

Scott got frustrated by his unintelligible tirade. Scott slapped him across the face, "ANSWER ME!"

With a force of a MAC Truck the bum was knocked into a pile-over of trash. The bum moaned as he struggled to get to his feet but could not.

The Scott saw him. His eyes were unnatural. No human eyes can emit light; a low burning glow. His eyes shone a beautiful verde. His mouth spread across his face in a maniacal, saber-toothed smile.

"How drunk am I?" Scott thought to himself.

"I do believe I am who you are looking for," The Dead Thing said.

Scott quickly swung a misguided punch; the vampire telegraphed the attack. "My, my, aren't we feisty. Who shoved that habanera up *your* ass?"

"Who the *fuck* are you," Scott said putting up his fist.

"You're a real tough guy," Aryk said. "Picking on the old and deranged. I'm confident you will be cutting the break line of bus full of special needs kids next."

"Come on asshole; I'll fuck you up!"

Aryk was never a fan of profanity when it's overused. "You know I would take that threat seriously if I were, well, alive," Aryk said. "Who else isn't alive..." Aryk paused, closing his eyes in an animiated fashion. One who loves to be dramatic when he kills Aryk couldn't help but taunt Scott before muttering in a mock sympathetic tone, "oh yeah: *Cecil.*"

Enraged Scott attacked the vampire who, ever gracefully, evaded the attack. Aryk spun around like a ballerina after an erroneous attempt of a tackle by

Scott. Aryk toyed with him; he always appreciated a good challenge.

He's good, Aryk thought. *If he wasn't so shit face he would have at least grazed me.* At that very moment a thunderous left was delivered to Aryk's face. He was shocked; he could not even remember the last time a mortal was ever fast enough to land a punch on him.

Scott's fist hurt – Aryk's flesh was unlike anything he had felt.He was ice; like hitting a stone wall in New York during the month of January. Scott put his fist back up and was ready to fight again.

"You're *FUN*," The Vampire said. "It's been a long time since one of you could actually lay a finger on me. I'm going to have fun with you before you die." Aryk then did something amazing, he echoed Brad Pitt's voice and said, "I want you to hit me as hard as you can."

Scott charged Aryk; he pulled out every trick his training taught him. Punches and kicks, however all of them missed. The Vampires movement was unlike a human; it seems like he could anticipate the attack before it was delivered, this frustrated Scott who only fought harder. Then, with very little effort from The Vampire, Scott was back handed many feet away landing on his right side.

"Oh forgive me; broken ribs are a bitch to heal," The Dead Thing taunted. "You've got to tell me there is *more* than what you are displaying. So come now; give us a kiss."

Scott sprung to his feet and charged Aryk again and delivered a punch combination which the vampire easily disabled. The Vampire held Scott's fist with his cold grip, and with undead strength, he slowly craned Scott closer to him. His nose touched Scott's; He could feel the vampire's cold odorless breath. Scott was helpless in the Aryk's grip and the vampire only said one word-

"*Extraordinary.*"

And with that same strength the vampire pulled Scott to him and sank his fangs into Scott's neck and began to drink.

It was 11:11am, 9/13/2012. The room was dark; the curtains were closed. The bright California sun still seeped into the room under the curtains. Scott was in his bed at his Culver City apartment. Scott was confident that he could not have slept that long; because it was eleven o'clock which was his usual time to get up.

Scott was still dizzy, confused, and weakened. He was sure that something was wrong with his clock. He had slept an entire day. Scott touched his neck and two tiny holes, crusted over with a scab, were detected.

"The *FUCK*?!" Scott said.

"Don't touch the curtains," a voice said.

It was him, it was Aryk. He stood in the corner of his bedroom, blanketed by shadows. His eyes only had a small glimmer of its intensity the last time Scott saw him. His eyes peered deep into Scott; looking into his soul. Scott's eyes disengaged Aryk's – he didn't want to see. Aryk's fangs were hidden behind his soft pink lips; pushed into a small pout.

"How... You... you're not..." Scott said as he tried to structure a sentence in a cohesive manner.

"Oh, Scott," The Vampire said. "You put a lot of stress on yourself. I can tell by this episode of

Hoarders that you call an apartment. Sit back, and let's chat a little."

"Who are you," Scott asked.

"How rude of me; I am Aryk Isaac Killen. But that doesn't answer much does it. Not like I'm listed in the Yellow Pages. I am on Twitter, however. Ask the *real* question."

"What are you?"

"Add it up it: two tiny holes in your neck, the fangs; it's not rocket science. You *know* what I am."

"What do you want?'

"Now *that's* the ten billion dollar question: What do I want?" Aryk took his right index finger and then took a small nipple. Aryk showed his bleeding finger to Scott, "it can't be *your* blood; I've had that – not too impressed either."

A dark smile crept across Aryk's face, "The *real* question is: what I can do *for* you. I can bring you to the vampire who took you sister's life. More importantly I've figured you out – you are sick of this mortal coil bullshit. You need eight pills a day to keep you from insanity but every day you inch closer and closer to it."

Scott sat himself up in his bed to get a better look at Aryk. The sudden movement caused a wave of pain rocked his body. Scott was drained of his blood and heavily weakened but he wanted to peer into Aryk's eyes with the same intensity as Aryk did him.

"You want it – you want your life back."

"You can give that to me."

Aryk chuckled at the mortals sincerity, "Of course not. We aren't life creating vessels. What I can do is give you something better. I can give you eternity."

"Why?" Scott said in a hoarse almost inaudible tone.

"Because I like you," Aryk said with a growing smirk. "You are the first mortal in a long time that could lay a finger on me. I find that absolutely-" Aryk paused for a second to find just the word to describe the phenomenon that was Scott, "-delicious.

"I've killed many, many mortals. And they pretty much all die the same; like fish out of water, just flopping around until their little gills can't breathe anymore. But *you* brought passion back to the game. You made things electric."

"*Game?*" Scott was confused. This creature spoke about life and death as if it was all pieces on a board but to Aryk it was. In the world of Aryk he was God and he decided who lived and who didn't.

"So here's where you make the choice: I can give you the vampire who killed Cecil but you would have to give me your life."

"What do you mean by: '*giving* you my life.'"

"Nothing's free, Scotty-O. Besides, you can't live in this mortal world anymore knowing what you know. If I were to leave you right now you wouldn't stop seeking vampires until one of them kills you and that would be a waste. Most vampires today wouldn't be able to see the potential in you I see."

"What do you need me to do," Scott asked in a determined voice.

"Change your sheets; you've pissed on yourself... again. Next, meet me in Korea Town behind the HoJo at 9:29 pm. Don't be late." Aryk scanned the room and focused his attention to the glowing sun attempting to breach the curtains. "Sunny day."

"I thought vampires slept in the day," Scott stated.

"Boy," Aryk began with a smile, "You got a lot to learn about, *vampires*."

And in an instant Aryk vanished into a dark fog; he dispursed like vapors, disenigrating into oblivion. As if he was never there at all.

"THE *FUCK*, man?!" Scott said. It was too early in the morning for this shit. Scott went to his night stand that was position right next to his bed. Scott grabbed his bottle of Jim Bean and started his day with a drink. He also pulled out his nine millimeter - he knew tonight was about to suck, immensely.

Rosewood, Florida

Aryk sat on his marble floor, legs crossed, hands on his knees; open palmed. His position was meditative; and at peace. Slowly, ever so slowly, blood trickled down his right nostril. Without warning Aryk coughs up a mist blood that breaks his meditative trance.

"What are you doing?" Angelique asked with a tone of disappointment.

"You would think after years I would be able to master this without -" Aryk paused and looked at his ruined floors, "the mess."

"And again I ask: what *are* you doing?"

"Astral Projection."

Angelique looked at Aryk with a bewildered stare.

"Astral projection is ability to send one's metaphysical self to anywhere on the physical and sometimes astral plane without moving one's physical body."

"Is that a vampire thing?" Angelique asked.

"Anyone can do it," Aryk said. "Everyone can't do it well."

Angelique scanned the blood that splattered against the floor. She sucked her teeth and teased,"Doesn't look like you're doing it all too well,."

Aryk smiled. "You're fun for a mortal."

"I'm the best thing you got going for you," Angelique declared.

Aryk thought for a second and then concurred, "You're right; you are. How pathetic is that?"

"Are you hungry?" she asked.

"Yes, a little."

As Angelique went to go fetch Aryk some fresh O-Negative blood from the fridge, he pondered. Aryk had been alone for many years, having a vampire partner could be just what he needed. It had been a long time since Aryk really enjoyed anything related to being a vampire, and a new birth could bring back the fire to this hellish marriage Aryk has with eternity.

Angelique warmed the blood by placing the glass jar holding the blood in a pot of boiling water. This was done so the blood would be warm but would not coagulate or burn. When she returned to where Aryk had sat, Aryk was nowhere to be seen.

"I'm in my study!" he said.

The home was pretty large and hidden in the forest. The outside of the house was rundown and covered in vines. The inside had been completed reinforced with steel and updated with modern technology and furniture.

Aryk's study looked like any other study; the walls were covered in books and a roaring fire blazed from the fireplace. Aryk was read a book, it appeared old and tattered from years and different owners. Aryk loved fireplaces; vampires' bodies are generally room temperature, so a fire kept him warm.

Angelique sat the tray holding his warmed jar of blood, a mug, and small bowl of nightshade. Nightshade is a poisonous herb used often in magic, particularly curses. Aryk enjoyed breaking pieces of nightshade into his blood; he says he like the effect it brings him.

Aryk sat quietly and rather studiously as he read the book. After wiping away dripping sweat from her forehead Angelique looked from a far at the leather bound old book.

"What's that?" Angelique asked.

"Noctosium," Aryk said. "Call it the modern vampire how-to manual."

"First of all, *modern*?" Angelique said placing her hand on her hip. "That book gotta be at least one hundred years old. And oh yeah, don't you know everything about being a vampire anyhow?"

"Three actually," Aryk corrected. "I am beyond a vampire. I transcended that many years ago. I am by far the most dominant vampire in this country."

"*But...*"

"I never turned a mortal before," Aryk said, rather shyly.

"Hahhahaha," Angelique said. "So what are you doing; studying?" Angelique continued to laugh at the notion that a vampire of Aryk's status would need to study on how to create another vampire.

Aryk let out a low growl and his green eyes began to glow angrily, "Do not mock me." Aryk was embarrassed; to not have changed a mortal is the equivalence of being a virgin. To not share the sacred blood, to not procreate at his age is actually, in the world of vampires, humiliating.

Angelique caught herself; family or not, Aryk was still a vampire. "Sorry about that, I just thought it was common knowledge. You drink, they drink, and then they're a vampire."

"Hate to take piss on your vampire mythology, but it's a lot more complicated than that," Aryk said as he turned the page. "Most humans will not survive the transformation if you don't do it immediately."

Aryk turned the page. "I found someone who I want to turn but I have already fed from him. His body is still connected to the mortal world but he has yet to drink from me. He is a hybrid."

"What happens to hybrids?"

"If not turned they eventually go insane."

"Why?"

"Well," Aryk began, "according to this book, hybrids are imbued with strength that most mortals don't posses. Not as strong as a vampire, but indeed powerful. Most of these hybrids eventually become vampire's hunters. Their minds are tormented by the face of the vampire who drank from them."

"The likelihood of a human running into the same vampire twice in their lives is extremely rare; so they spend their lives hunting them. That is their ultimate fantasy."

"So what makes this one so special that you not only let them live, but you plan to turn him?"

"Because he started searching for me, specifically. No bite required. Someone like that I can't ignore. So tonight we will have his audition, I didn't guarantee the part to him just yet."

"This isn't a movie," Angelique said.

"To me it is," Aryk said as he poured himself a mug of blood.

This was indeed a movie; the idea of entertainment for a bored immortal. Aryk had no intention on standing Scott up and he was confident Scott had no intentions on not showing up.

"And he should be happy," Aryk began, "he was chosen."

Chapter

6

Late Summer 2012

7:48pm

Skid Row, Los Angeles

A red bow covered Aryk mouth after he snatched away from the transient. A blissful smile was etched across his face before he sucked in air meaninglessly. The man coughed and gargles on his own blood, Aryk feeling charitable finished it with a snap. Aryk dropped the homeless chap to the ground and dusted of his clothes.

Skid Row is not safe for anyone in LA, except vampires. Aryk loved this city, it was such a contradiction. The City of Angels was far from angelic or heavenly. Besides vampire, Los Angeles was plagued with every other boogieman there was. But more than vampires, mortals were the most ruthless.

Aryk was banking on that; especially in Scott's viciousness. He could taste it in his blood – the vampire was confident that darkness existed in him. Darkness, Aryk has it and he could feel it in Scott too. Aryk was not sure yet if he would turn him. Many vampire masters create fledglings solely for ego. Many vampire masters had an army of vampire servants they conceived.

Aryk did not want all of that, he only desired excitement. So many years had passed since Scarlett was ripped from his arms. Ninety-two years and the wounds were just as fresh. Aryk mused on how the beautiful vampire would run nude, wildly through the forest –his moon nymph.

But Aryk quickly banished thoughts of Scarlett. Today was 2012, and no amount of reminiscing would bring her back.

Aryk knew he had enough time to visit Venice Beach to watch the eccentric humans perform on the streets. Aryk enjoyed the different performances; his otherworldliness blended well with theirs. Aryk relaxed his body and used his vampiric powers to defy gravity – like a shooting star he flew across the night sky.

Century City, Los Angeles

Scott stared intensely in the mirror. Scott wanted to imprint his image into his mind forever – as far as he knew, today would be the last time he would see it – his reflection By now Scott had accepted that Aryk was indeed a vampire. He had to be, because if he was not then Scott was truly losing his mind. That would be a true tragedy, the lost of one sibling sending a war veteran into an angry rage then finally a psychotic breakdown.

Get it together Scott, he encouraged to himself. He wanted to call his therapist, Sergeant O'Bryan. He would say that the depression from his sister's death has caused rebound psychosis. In short he was losing his mind and he did not want to hear that shit.

Scott searched through his closet for the right ensemble; he was still a valley boy at heart. He never got rid of all his v-necks t-shirts and Diesel Jeans. It reminded him of a time where life was simple; the real question was could he still fit any of his old cloths anymore.

How does one get ready to die? You should probably ask the hundreds of men on death row in America. But Scott had an idea. He understood that life could be extinguished quickly with out a trace of warning.

Everyday Scott thought he could have died while in Iraq and in a very general way he was right. Everyday could be your last, war or no war. Life in itself is a war and casualties happen more often than not.

Scott refused to be a causality. He had survived too much. But today he was offered eternal life by what he believed to be a vampire. To never be touched by old age or sickness ever again. To remain young, powerful, and in the prime of his life for all time; quite the enticing offer.

It had to be true. Scott settled on black jeans and navy blue v-neck; he strapped a 9 millimeter on his ankle along with hunting knife. Scott was not going to be stupid. Just in case this vampire gets too frisky, Scott put on his silver crucifix. Now, he was ready.

Scott's phone began to ring and "SuperBass" by Nicki Minaj filled the air, cutting the all so serious mood he forced himself in. Beth demanded that be her ringer even though it screamed gay. But Scott had very few male friends –or friends at all for that matter. He wasn't too in touch with ringtone etiquette, he silences his phone.

He just didn't have time for Beth. This was bigger than her. Scott prayed that he would be delivered from this life and perhaps he could bring Beth with him. But not tonight, tonight his focus was on himself and getting closer to the truth about Cecil.

Korean Town, Los Angeles

It was getting cold. Early fall in LA usually was if you consider a seventy six degree nights as cold. Korea Town had simplicity to it; it did not strive for the pseudo-authentic vibe that China Town did. The lovely locals walked up the uneven streets wearing Korean couture dresses and expensive pumps. The aroma of Asian cuisine permeated in the air. The air smelled of fried rice being prepared by the Chinese restaurant up the street, but the smell of crack cocaine being lit by a junkie in the alley could also be sensed.

All those succulent mortal treats.

The HoJo was placed right in the middle of it.

Los Angeles had the most glamorous to the most dismal areas. The place had style, characters, and creatures. Creatures like vampires. Which are, by the way, the most deadly.

Aryk deviousness is well documented. His heinous acts are often boasted at vampire parties thrown usually at churches. Many of these churches masquerade as Christian but are often satanic in root. Aryk was popular but loathed his fame in the world of the undead.

Scott pulled out Newport cigarettes and lit one. Aryk watched from a hotel rooftop. A vampire's vision is greater than any animals at night. The night is the source of vampires' vampiric power.

Aryk analyzed Scott; he wanted to know which Scott he would get. Would he get the strong, bash, soldier or would he get the fragile, shell-shocked shadow of his former self? Or would he get that other thing; the monster that hid under the skin of Scott?

Aryk was confident it was there all it needed was a little encouragement.

Scott's body language displayed a scared youth who was far from out of his realm of understanding. He looked pathetic –so pathetic Aryk wondered if killing him would be the most merciful thing to do. But Aryk wasn't much for mercy."You shouldn't smoke those – you'll get crow's feet," Aryk said after landing noiselessly in front of Scott.

Scott was frightened, he had never seen anyone jump from so high and land with grace and poise. He could not show fear if he did Scott was sure Aryk would not turn him. "If tonight goes well," Scott said with a small shake in his voice, "I won't need to worry about that."

A small smirk appeared on the Dead Thing's face, Aryk appreciated the saucy response. But he could still smell the fear on Scott – he was bathed in it. "You made it," Aryk said to Scott as he stood alone in the parking garage under the hotel.

Scott was suspicious, suspicious of himself. Scott knew he had to be crazy; there was no way he was not.

Scott did not trust himself, how could he when talking about vampires and promises of immortality. Scott asked Aryk. "How do I know I'm not crazy? How do I know this isn't just-"

"An illusion?" Aryk completed. "I'm sure you get a lot those with your-" Aryk caught himself and pondered for the most *appropriate* terminology, "*handicap.*"

"I'm not retarded," Scott shot back with venom.

"Nor are you very politically correct."

In a demanding voice Scott exclaimed, "How do I know? I need to know if this – if any of this is real."

Scott began make steps backwards; terror had truly set in. Scott was faced with real evil; not some Government Appointed Evil he was brainwashed into believing. True evil. True darkness.

"Don't be afraid," Aryk taunted, we're all friends here." Aryk smiled at the idea of just feeding on Scott. But that act would not be very fruitful. Aryk was a god, and like the greek gods before him he wanted to test the mortal.

"This is your one and only opportunity to receive a power that no mortal could ever give you. All your life you have felt your potential was being wasted – and it was. Tonight you will see what very few ever get to see – the power of true vampire. And if you are worthy you will be made."

Aryk gave the mortal a fanged smile before leading him out of the alley into the sea of people.

Aryk was always two steps ahead of Scott. Aryk could feel the tension in Scott's body. He could feel his blood pressure pulsating every time the small space between them was threatened. Aryk had not spent a lot of time with mortals outside of Angelique. But unlike Scott, Angelique had lived with Aryk her entire life. He was family to her.

Aryk listened to the rhythm of Scott's heartbeat – it pulsated at an irregular pace. Aryk deduced it was an undiagnosed heart condition. Aryk could smell Scott – all humans have a similar musk. Similar however distinct; Aryk could smell Scott cologne mixed with his own body oils. A vampire never misses a scent.

Scott told Aryk everything he needed to know without speaking. The vampire was unable to read mind and had only limited telepathy, he did poses the power of empathy – to sense a creatures emotions.

More important than what one is thinking is what one is feeling. Banishing thoughts are easy, but hiding emotions are not.

Aryk could smell the rotting scent of fear. It oozed from his pores – sliding down his face before he wipes it away from his eyes. Saline flavored grime. However sometimes fear brings the best out of a creature. *Humans are known to perform great feats under shadow fear so perhaps this won't be a waste of my time.*

Scott was too terrified to walk side by side with Aryk. For starters, he was a vampire; a mythical, bloodsucking, fiend from legend. The reality had sunk in when he laid eyes on Aryk again. Aryk was indeed a vampire. It made Scott contemplate what else was out there.

Scott figured if he stayed a step or two from Aryk he could never be taken by surprise. Aryk may not have been an illusion; but that made things worst. Abilify can treat illusions but does not do shit to vampires, unfortunately.

Vampires live forever – they see everything. We only read about historical events but Dead Things they actually live in it. Scott had so many questions, his mind became overloaded with queries that he began to lose Aryk already brisk pace.

His curiosity empowered his courage and so he asked, "How old are you?"

"Haven't you heard that a rude question to ask?" Aryk's voice was Antarctic. His voice was dry; the wetness of life was missing from his tone. Scott paid attention to the numerous differences between himself and Aryk. "Watch and learn."

Aryk closed his green eyes and dipped his head back. The Dead thing took a quick sniff. He could not find his target. He could sense Scott emotional tailspin. *Humans; they can never keep their feelings in order.* Scott emotional interference was making it harder for Aryk to sense his targets.

"I was born 1831; Virginia." Scott ears perked with excitement. "And being a mulatto in those days was interesting."

"Were you a slave?" before the words could escape his mouth Aryk grabbed the human by his throat and pinning him to the wall. His fangs exposed, threatening to ravage Scott.

"Figlio di puttana! The vampire hissed at Scott holding him inches off his feet.

Scott gargled on his explanation – he wanted to tell him that historically... he just assumed. The vampire pulled him closer to his animalistic mouth. "I am from a class and society that your obtuse human mind could never comprehend."

"I'm sorry," Scott forced out of his constricted throat. Aryk quickly released him allowing him to fall on the filth covered Los Angeles pavement. The snob in Aryk emerged, and like a dandy he dusted invisible dust from his clothes. "You're very disrespectful, Scott. Not only did you insult me – you used a rather old insult."

"I'm sorry – just historically."

"The thing is its history to you," Aryk's voiced trailed as he began again to track his target. "Once you live through *history* then you'll know."

"You've seen everything haven't you?" Scott wanted to know more, so he stroked Aryk's ego. He hopes such a question would make Aryk tell him more.

Aryk could sense the fox in his henhouse. But it did yield results; the vampire was in a charitable mood so he fed Scott the morsel of attention he desired.

"Others have seen more," Aryk flat voice was smooth. "But so have you."

"I've seen death – it changes people."

With a dark grin Aryk replied "You've killed people – that changes people too."

"You feed on them," Scott defiantly shot back.

"I feed to exist however you fed the greed of a nation with the blood of innocent people. Who's the real monsters?"

Aryk was being evasive, and Scott could tell. Scott could tell by the peaks and valleys in Aryk's voice. Aryk could tell that Scott was scanning him; reading his body language.

Aryk actually loved it; he loved the initiative Scott took. He was ballsy for a human. Most human let their terror take over but Scott found a way to channel it. Aryk was curious to see how Scott's human nature would translate to vampire instinct.

Much of one's humanity is lost once a human is embraced by a vampire. The magic of evolution happens and they become a child of the night – a Dead Thing. The dead feeds off the essence of the living because they cannot produce life.

Aryk had never had a child before. Aryk saw himself dimly shine through this mortal's eyes. Aryk's dark powers had mildly enhanced Scott through the bite he received Being under the thrall of a Dead Thing has its advantages, mildly enhanced abilities and connection to the astral world.

For Mortals, child birth requires a man and a woman, or a shit load of science. But for vampires, one vampire can *conceive* an infinite number of *infants*. The only two elements needed is the Bite and the mystical blood that courses through vampires.

Aryk stopped mid-step and began to sniff around like a hare. Aryk cut his eyes to the left and then took in another whiff.

"He' s here."

"Who?"

"Try to keep up," Aryk said faintly before with blurring speed shot through the large group of people. Scott was mystified; the fact that Aryk could move so fast was already outrageous. But the notion of Scott keeping up was even more ludicrous. And where the hell was he going anyhow?

"Come on Scott, let's go!" Aryk's voice echoed in Scott's mind, bouncing of the walls of his

consciousness. The voice was maddening. Scott couldn't stand straight, body was taken over by the voice –the pressure in his brain almost brought Scott to his knees.

Scott ran through the crowd bumping into numerous people and was usually greeted with a "fuck you" or two. Scott's stomach turned as he got closer to the alley behind a Mobile gas station. He knew wherever he needed to find was there.

Scott quickly stopped when he reached the Alley where Aryk stood talking with another male. He could tell that this would not be a friendly confrontation. Scott could still feel the pressure in his brain from Aryk's telepathic message but his focus remained on the mysterious male.

"You walk around this town like you're royalty," male voice said coming from deeper in the alley.

"Come now, Vahn," Aryk said. "There is a pecking order, I'm sorry that even with your age you don't have as much clout as me."

"The vampires of this area are getting sick and tired of you, boy. I got a lot of years on you and enough power to rip you apart."

"*Threats*," Aryk said with a condescending drag to his voice. "Those are never useful."

Scott finally could see the man; he looked in his mid thirties but Scott knew he was like Aryk, a vampire. The man's skin was pale with a tint of blue to add a morgue-esque look. His eyes had a tint of insanity to them as if at any moment he could erupt.

"You are a *vapor* to me!" The man's voice boomed with outrage and anger. "I rose from the ashes of Rome and became a god of this new world. You have yet to reach my pedestal."

Aryk enjoyed the monologue, he found it very old school. "Congratulations –I am intimidated."

"*Aryk*," Scott called out nervously.

"You brought a fucking human to this meeting," The vampire asked Aryk who stood there quietly and emotionless with a bored, Walter Cronkite stare. "He better be a fucking peace offering or-"

With lightening speed, Aryk forced his hand through the vampire's chest. Fangs exposed on both vampires, Vahn fell to his knees while Aryk caught him by throat.

"Someone's fangs are really growing in," Aryk taunted as he tightened his grip mercilessly. "A vampire must learn a lot after he is made, but Scott's lucky, Vahn. He will be familiar with destroying blood rats like yourself before he's even a vampire."

Coughing through his wound and blood Vahn chuckled, "You can't think your human will survive this."

Aryk drug Vahn's bleeding face closer to his, and with a dark hiss to his ear Aryk replied, "I know you're not."

Three shadowy clouds appeared behind Vahn and with a hard push knocked Aryk away. Aryk rolled and tumbled to his feet with an agile grace. Crimson, icy drops of blood slithered down his nostrils. The blood was absorbed back into Aryk skin leaving an unstained finish.

Vahn powers of regeneration had already begun as he was almost completely healed. Older vampire's have this skill. Vahn had all but regained his full vigor and was ready to punish Aryk. "I think I'll start with your mortal."

Aryk gleamed at the group of vampires aligned against him. He always loved a good challenge and what better challenge than a battle of vampires. "Now that's what I like to see," Aryk said with an acid hiss.

The shadows had slowed down and expose three female vampires; dressed in satin dresses with porcelain faces and platinum blonde tresses. All except one – her skin was of browned caramel but her face was just as smooth and angelic as her sisters.

Stand back, Scott, Aryk said telepathically.

Scott's processed the message with booming invasion. A mortal's mind is not designed for telepathic communication. Aryk had not mastered the art of telepathy and his powers overwhelmed Scott's still human mind.

"Fuck!" Scott cried out. "Can you stay the *hell* out of my head?

Keep QUIET!, Aryk responded, telepathically causing Scott to cry out again.

Noticing the moment of weakness, the four vampires attacked Aryk, whom was momentarily distracted. The first to reach was the ebony skinned female vampire; Aryk quickly snatched her by the face and repelled her into the large steel garbage pins that lined the alley.

The second wave of assaults was conducted by Vahn and his two female partners; Aryk easily over powered the female vampires but Vahn proved to be closer to him in power.

Scott was frozen; he could not take his eyes off the fight he was too transfixed by the battle. *They move so different*-he thought. The female vampires fought like bobcats; scratching and clawing at Aryk. Vahn was more like a cougar; he used his strength along with his speed. But Aryk was the *il lupo* – the wolf. He dismissed the attacks by the girls with very little effort. But with Vahn, Scott could see Aryk had to use all of his enormous power.

Scott was also frozen in place for another reason; because Aryk willed it so. Once a vampire has bitten you, you are under his influence until *that* vampire is destroyed or releases you.

The once disposed vampire had risen to her feet and began to stalk the brawl. As she inched closer to the fight, she hungrily anticipated a point of entry.

"Behind you, Aryk" Scott cried out.

But even before Scott spoke, Aryk could sense the words filling Scott's mind. With a thunderous roundhouse kick, Aryk sent the assailant flying into Scott's direction.

She landed on the pavement, face first. The small scratches that marred her face became visible as she rose to her feet. Her lip snarled when her eyes locked on to Scott.

Scott wanted to run, but his feet were still frozen by Aryk's hypnotic influences. Aryk could sense Scott's terror rise; without words, Aryk released Scott from the tar like mental hold.

Instinct kicked in and Scott attempted to run but the female vampire cut him off. Desperate to escape Scott ran the opposite direction. Using her amazing speed she cut Scott off again.

"No more running," she said in a soft Carrabin accent. "You die."

Fight or die, son, Aryk's voice boomed through Scott's mind. Befuddled, Scott put up his fist. But he could not do it; he simply could bring himself to hit a woman.

"Oh," she said with a glowing swoon, "such a gentleman." And like a wrecking ball, her fist sent Scott flying feet away. "And who said chivalry was dead?"

The vampire enjoyed knocking around Scott. Even though male gender roles are voided in the world of vampires, she enjoyed over powering the much larger male.

Scott was too slow to return to his feet before another onslaught was delivered. Lefts and rights, the maniacal vampire delivered unforgiving blows to Scott's face.

Sensing the plight of his potential progeny, Aryk quickly reaches into his back pocket and retrieved a small golden blade. Between knocking out all his opponents with a thunderous roundhouse, Aryk hurled the blade at the cocoa skinned vampire. Like a dart hitting its bull's eye the blade imbedded itself into the vampire's face.

She screamed in horror as her icy blood spurted from the gash. It was all real. The violence, the blood, all of it was real. Scott's mind began to be assaulted with memories of his military tour. He could hear their cries again –he could smell the burning buildings. The senselessness of it all had returned.

FOCUS, Aryk's voice boomed in Scott's mind. *"You need to capitalize."*

Aryk had made a way for Scott to turn this fight around and Scott knew that if he did not take a stand now he would die. Still trapped in a flash back –Scott warrior nature took over.

With his left hand, Scott removed the blade from the face of the vampire and using the same momentum he drove the blade deep into the gut of the vampire.

The blade cut deep, so deep that the steel handle was no longer visible. She gasped in horror. Her eyes were pained with terror. She began to shake wildly and violently as she vomited blood. Small embers began to expels from her mouth.

She desperately clawed at her stomach in an attempt to pry loose the blade. Finally over taken, she falls to the ground and shatters into pieces. Small crystal shards were red coated lightly with blood. She was dead, broken into pieces it was as if she was never there..

So that's how they look when they die, Scott pondered mutely. Aryk smiled back at Scott –pride swelled in Aryk's chest. Scott had no idea what he had just accomplished. This proved what Aryk suspected all along –Scott was worthy.

"ROXANNA!" Vahn cried out as his offspring shattered bleeding nothingness.

Aryk's power was massive, far more superior to Vahn. Desperation began to seep into Vahn's heart. "You *and* your mortal are gonna burn," Vahn in a low sour growl.

Scott, get behind me, commanded Aryk telepathically. Scott stumbled to his feet desperately before running over to Aryk. Aryk could feel it coming, in every one of his cells he could sense the onslaught that was approaching. Aryk summoned his vampire powers and braced himself for the attack.

Vahn's eyes changed from a soft glowing blue to a deep crimson. The once teal veins licked across his skin turned black and his hands begin to tremble as he conjured his powers.

"You've got a long time before you can reach my power," Vahn declared.

A flash of blinding light expelled from the Vahn's hands. The flash brought Scott to his knees but Aryk stood like a statue without blinking or turning away. A globe of flames danced in Vahn's hand, hissing and scorching the air.

Vahn had summoned fire which is a tall order for vampires and Aryk knew Vahn could not maintain this level of power for long.

"I may not have *your* power," Aryk said scaling the alley for a way of his predicament. "Guess, I'll just have to be smarter."

"Say hi to Scarlet for me," Vahn said before hurling the flaming mass at Aryk.

"Do you have a plan?" Scott asked.

"Not really," Aryk lied.

Scott dug and in pocket and removed his trump card –he removed a small grenade. And with a strong toss Scott threw the frag at Vahn, one of Vahn's women attempted to catch the grenade but inadvertently detonated the explosive. Aryk's eyes dilated as his put his right hand forward grabbing Scott and lifting him into the air avoiding the explosion. The fire quickly engulfed Aryk's foes as vampires are highly susceptible to fire.

Aryk wanted to see, he wanted to watch Vahn burn. Aryk settled on the roof of neighboring building and landed there with Scott. Scott was shaken by the explosion and again by being lifted into the air without warning.

Vahn desperately tried to gain control of the inferno but the flames overpowered him. The fire spread throughout the alley, burning trash and neighboring building. Aryk became stimulated by the death of his foes –Dead Things always appreciate destruction. Scott however was horrified to watch creatures suffer, even evil ones.

Aryk stood still. He was frozen by his own powers. By tapping into his still developing powers he became paralyzed. Aryk was transfixed by his own will as well as the flames. But the fire was getting out of control, other buildings were on fire now. The fire had reached the building where Scott and Aryk stood.

"Aryk," Scott called out. The inferno became too much for the mortal to bare. Scott wanted to run, all his instincts screamed for him to run. But he could not leave Aryk.

Something bound Scott to Aryk and the thought of Aryk being destroyed in the fire was too much for Scott to take. Scott grabbed Aryk and pulled him away from the blazing fire. Aryk was then released from the hold he was under.

Aryk's eyes locked with Scott's and he saw her. Cecil. Scott's and Cecil had the same eyes, the same look of horror.

"It's time to go," Scott declared.

Chapter

7

"Can all vampires do that?" Scott asked Aryk as they moved further away from the fire.

Aryk was drained; even vampires at Aryk's level have limits. Aryk did not want to show his weak side to anyone, especially someone he plans to make a fledgling. But he needed to feed. As Scott asked a river of questions, Aryk looked for the perfect victim.

"Aryk, are you listening," Scott asked.

"I can hear you," Aryk finally responded. "And if you keep talking at this volume, so will everyone else."

Aryk could sense the mortals around him attention being aroused by Scott's voice. Besides there being a large fire roaring behind them Aryk did not need any more unwanted attention. So Aryk did what he figured was the best thing to do.

"We need to leave, little brother," Aryk said. Aryk slipped pass the mass of people gawking at the fire. Scott was on his heels following Aryk into another alley.

Then the vampire stopped. Scott had so many questions, so much he needed to understand before he could move any further. Aryk could sense Scott's suspicions; he could see the queries bounce around in Scott's brain before reached his mouth.

"Aryk – "

With one figure the vampire hushed Scott. "This isn't over by a long shot. We still have much to do."

Santa Monica, CA

The Loew Beach Hotel had five star accommodations; Dead Things like Aryk always have to ride in style. The room was modernized with the top of the line French furniture and linen. The aroma of apple cider permeated in the air. Hip artwork lined the walls along with flat screen televisions. The 3 bedroom suite was usually rented by celebrities but today royalty lived there. Well, perhaps *live* isn't the best word to use.

Scott stood alone on the balcony and watched the ocean meet and retract from the shore. Cecil's voice entered his mind –*Jonas brothers are gay*. He smiled as the memory of Cecil rejecting his Jonas Brothers CD, he was confident that secretly she loved them.

Aryk waited patiently for his guest to arrive. She was late –*Isn't delivery free if it's thirty minutes late?* Aryk laughed to himself, he truly cracked himself up. Breaking his private joke was a knock at the door.

The buxom brunette smiled when she saw Aryk. He was stall, soft olive skin, soft beautiful full lips. He was beautiful, *score!* In the world of prostitution a girl had to kiss many frogs but today she got a prince.

"I'm Candy," she said with a smile.

Aryk couldn't help but lick his lips at the sight of her body –it was quite the morsel. "Yes you are, aren't you." He took her hand and led her into the hotel.

She marveled at the beauty of the room, now this is what she was talking about. Janice, her madam, had sent her to enough shit holes. This was more like it. Aryk offered her wine –she eagerly accepted.

Scott could hear commotion in the suite, it was a female's voice –a familiar voice. Scott was astounded when he saw Shelly in the hotel room. Shelly was shocked to see Scott there as well. She seductive smiled as it dawned on her, *He was just playing hard to get earlier.*

Aryk was curious to see the reaction they would give each other and know he knew. "Are you familiar with my friend," Aryk asked with false naivety.

"Not at all," she said with a dark grin.

"Good," he said with hardy tone. He then cut his eyes to Shelly again licking his lips desperately holding back his fangs, "Shall we."

"Right here, right now," she asked.

"Why not?"

"I'm just used to –its fine."

Aryk used his fingers to release the buttons on his shirt; one by one each button sprang free until his chest was freed. Shelly/Candy took the initiative to plant a wet kiss on Aryk before grabbing his package —she was vulgar, and Aryk loved it. He skin felt oddly colder against her lips, so much the she drew back.

"Don't," Aryk responded before pulling her closer for another kiss. She melted in Aryk's arms, never before had she experienced such passion from a date. It felt more than just business, she felt loved.

Shelly pulled away from the kiss and with one smooth motion she removed her short figure hugging dress. Her breast stood happily and youthfully at attention. Her skin was smooth, tanned, unblemished. She was indeed the picture of perfection, indeed Aryk's type.

He suggested she move to the couch where Scott stood watching. Something was rising in Scott, an urge like none before. It was greater than sex, it was stronger than hunger, Scott had a desire to feed.

She laid nude on the couch as the vampire performed oral sex on Shelly. Her knew wobbled with the excitement as the vampire teased her with his skills. She grabbed him by the back of his head before letting out a orgasmic sigh, "Where the fuck did you learn that?"

Aryk couldn't help but smile, "You taste..." the vampire then exposed his fangs and bit quickly into femoral artery. Shelly screamed out as the Dead Thing sucked but then quickly stopped and smiled, "cheap."

"Oh my god," Scott screamed as he watched the blood drip from Aryk's mouth. "What are you doing?"

"You said you wanted eternity," Aryk said. "*THIS* is eternity."

"You can't kill her."

"Oh yes I can," Aryk challenged. "But I'm not, you are."

Shelly screamed out as blood gushed from between her legs, she attempted to flee but was quickly overpowered by Aryk who pinned her right back to the couch. Annoyed by her scream Aryk with ease covered her mouth, muting her screams.

"We don't have all day," Aryk prompted Scott. "This is how it's done."

"I can't kill her," Scott refused.

"The venom of my bite will only last in you so long –soon you will be just a mediocre mortal. To be reborn you must abandon your humanity. You must feed, now!"

Scott noticed that Aryk could not simply force him. Whatever thrall Aryk had over Scott could not force him to feed. "I won't do it."

"Fine, I will."

"Ok I believe!" Scott cried out desperately. "I believe that you are a vampire, I believe that you are real, just –just stop!"

Aryk quickly snatched Scott by his collar dragging his body into his embrace and dove his fangs into Scott's throat.

Los Angeles, California

"Scott..."

The sound of his name bounced around his mind but he was stuck in an abyss. The darkness enveloped Scott. It was as if he was no longer apart of the world. His essence was released into the mystical ether and his body laid lifeless on the earthly realm.

"Scott..."

A warm sensation tingled against his cold skin. The electricity shot through every nerve in his body. Without warning Scott popped up from his slumber.

The fast reaction startled Beth who had been trying to wake Scott up for the last five minutes.

Scott's eyes groggily scanned the area. He was in his room, in his bed. Scott climbed out his bed and ran to his mirror that was perched on his wall. Beth was confused watching Scott search his neck for wounds. His muscular neck was unblemished. No sign of Aryk's dark embrace; no trace of him anywhere.

"It had to be a dream," Scott said to himself.

"*What* was a dream?" Beth asked Scott. She was becoming increasing concerned; Scott's behavior had been erratic since he came back from Iraq. But after losing Cecil, Scott had become even more reclusive.

"Scott, I've called you for the last three days," Beth said to Scott who was still astonished by the now invisible bite. "Feel free to tell me what the *fuck* is going on."

Scott could hear Beth complaining, but he did not care. Whatever it was, it was nowhere near the importance as what happened to him. Scott knew the events that ensued over the last fews day were real. Aryk was real. But the only proof he had was the bite which now was gone.

He had to be real, Scott thought while Beth continue to go on and on about how she was so concerned about him. Scott's mind was only on Aryk.

"Are you even listening to me?" Beth exclaimed.

"Sorry," Scott apologized. Through the mirror Scott locked eyes with Beth's cascade eyes. "I've been really down, Beth. Since –"

"– I know." Beth walked behind her fiancé wrapping her arms around his waist. Her soft petal lips kissed his skin, electricity was sent through him again. "I'm here for you."

"I'll be ok," Scott said.

Beth put her face against Scott's skin; she inhaled the sweet musk of his body. She braced herself before telling Scott, "Sam and Vanna are dead."

"*What?*" Scott spun around to meet Beth's eyes. "How?"

"*Something* ate him and his wife," Beth said. "Sam and Vanna were found mauled to death."

"*God!*" Scott exclaimed. The sheer thought of a human being ate was a horrifying thought. Scott pondered for a second and then Aryk entered his mind again. *Could this be related?* "Were there marks, on their necks."

"*Morbid* much?" Beth said pulling away from Scott. She was taken aback from Scott's bizarre inquiry.

"I mean was it like an animal," Scott said, trying to mask his interest.

Beth was still freaked out, "I guess. I didn't ask to look at the bodies."

Realizing that he had seriously disturbed her Scott backpedaled to his normal personality as caring fiancé. "When's the funeral; has the family set up arraignments?"

"Not yet," Beth said. She took a deep breath, she knew what she would say next could complete freak her shell-shocked honey but she had work to do. "I need to go to Florida. He had some secret project that he wanted me to take care of. He entrusted me specially to take care of this."

"When are we leaving?" Scott asked, grasping her soft hand.

Rosewood, Florida

Aryk sat in his room alone brooding. Aryk was sure that Scott could be a great protégé. He had the wherewithal to be a superb vampire. But he was not ready, he would most likely never be. Aryk never took rejection or failure very well and Scott was both.

The Floridian sky was dark and gray due to the upcoming tropical storm. Days like this Aryk would be on his porch watching the semi lit sky. Even though it is technically daylight hours, Aryk could stand outside for a few hours before the sun would begin to affect him. But instead he was in his house feeling sorry for himself.

"Turn on the TV!" Angelique screamed from downstairs.

Aryk remain silent. No amount of *Robot Chicken* would make him feel better. But Angelique screamed out again for Aryk to turn on the television. Angelique galloped up the winding stairs desperately.

"What could possibly be on television that I need to see," Aryk asked in a low growl. "Is it 9/11 again?"

With the universal remote Angelique turned on the sixty inch plasma television:

The second mauling in three days in the Cedar Key area. Police suspect a wild animal most likely a panther was responsible...

"I know you're trying to make me feel better and usually a mauling would do the trick –"

"How many man-eating panthers do you know, Aryk?" Angelique asked.

"*Leopard of Rudraprayag*, killed hundreds of people in India," Aryk replied cold and bluntly, as if he was reading from an encyclopedia.

"First question: when's the last time have you seen a panther out here?" and before Aryk could give his rebuttal Angelique asked, "And panthers and cougars only hunt humans when there is a food shortage. You're telling me out of all the rabbits and deer a '*panther*' couldn't find food?"

Aryk processed the information. Angelique made a very provocative argument. "Ok, what are you expecting me to do? Grab my boom stick and hunt it down?"

Sarcasm was a luxury that Aryk rarely indulged in. Aryk did not seem very interested in the strange killings in his neighborhood. Aryk, like most vampires, are very territorial. But for some reason the thought of another supernatural creature killing people in his community did not seem to bother him much.

After receiving a disappointed scowl from Angelique the vampire yielded to his last remaining living descendant's badgering, "I'll check it out. I imagine it will give me something to do. I rarely get a chance to hunt at 3:00pm in the afternoon."

The clouds blocked out the sun but there was still a melancholy glow over the town of Cedar Key. Cedar Key was a small town, only a few miles from Aryk's Rosewood estate. And like many small rural Floridian towns, racial tensions were still present. And as a mulatto Aryk stuck out like a sore thumb.

It did not help that Aryk was dressed so flamboyant; with his short leather biker jacket, dark denim slacks, and matching black tank. His unnatural green eyes covered by dark Prada shades. The locals watched the vampire walk up Dock Street very closely. People that were flashy and non-white were a rarity in a small town like Cedar Key.

Aryk could smell something, and it was not human. It smelled primal and ancient; Aryk knew that this was no panther. Following his enhanced senses Aryk found the small home where the monster last attacked. Bright yellow tape was still wrapped around the trees; the smell was stronger the closer Aryk got. Aryk kept his eyes open for a possible surprise attack from whatever was causing these maulings.

The old house was slightly dilapidated and the tall grass made the home look all the more unattractive. With a quick push Aryk broke the lock and walked through the door.

"Hey you're not supposed to be –" The officer began before with lightening speed Aryk pinned him to the wall and fed off his blood. Aryk drained him dry and allowed his body to fall limply to the ground.

"*Rude,*" Aryk declared.

Refreshed, Aryk turned to look at the run down house. It could use a broom and mop. It was covered in filth and numerous odors, but Aryk was looking for a specific odor. And he found it; the scent that bathed the small town. Aryk searched the house for additional clues but all he could find was more the same odor.

Aryk was sure whatever it was had left and was long gone. Aryk did not want to bring any more attention to himself, besides he was sure if there was one officer there would be more. He would hate to have to slaughter the entire Cedar Key police department.

Aryk continued to follow the smell out the back door where the odor began to fade. "Well this was slightly uneventful," he complained aloud. But then something stood out. It was a small paw print. It was small and was not canine; the toes were too far apart and in a different position. Aryk was not familiar with this animal print.

Aryk softly dipped his finger into the print, making sure he did not disturb it. Aryk brought his fingers to his face and inhaled. The vampire cough and spat; it was indeed the monster in question foot imprint. Aryk removed his iPhone and snapped a picture of the imprint. Aryk texted the picture to a colleague of his along with the message:

"Get to Florida by sun fall."

Chapter

<u>8</u>

Gainesville, Florida

"Hey there," Beth said to Scott as he opened his eyes after the long flight to Florida. Scott took half an Ambien, halfway hoping to see Aryk in his dreams. He was hoping that Aryk would return and help him find out who killed Cecil like he promised. Aryk never arrived and his question remained unanswered.

"*Hey there*, back," he said with a small smirk. Beth kissed him softly on the lips before telling him she loved him.

They made it to Gainesville, Florida airport safely with no turbulence. Scott could feel something in the pit of his stomach. Something was very wrong, but knowing something was off Scott still continued.

"Scott, what time is it?" Beth asked.

Scott looked at his phone and replied, "4:25pm."

"We are looking at a two hour drive to Sumner," Beth confessed.

Scott finally stood as the rest of the passenger exited the plane. "Well, I have always been a fan of road trips. Plus, I love Florida."

"This isn't *South Beach*, babe," Beth teased. "We are going to the woods basically."

"Nice," Scott teased back. "I can commune with nature."

Beth gave him a playful punch to the arm, which she noticed was a lot harder than usual. "This isn't funny. I know you hate snakes, and I am sure I am going to run into at least one."

She had no idea how prophetic her words would be.

Sumner, Florida

The F-150 rental wobbled over the poorly paved road and it was beginning to make Beth sick to her stomach. They had driven over two hours to the small town of Sumner, Florida. It was beginning to take a toll on the couple. The GPS was going in and out of service and since Scott was the driver he had to rely on Beth questionable navigation skills.

"Why did they have to live in the middle of nowhere?" Scott complained. Scott was never a fan of nature or wild animals; he was a city boy and a spoiled one at that.

Beth was searching through her phone for her last text messages regarding the death her mentor. She attempted to ignore Scott's statement but he continued to complain about the unpaved roads and overgrown trees. So she chimed in, "He lives here because he wanted to commune with nature. Sam's feels because of the work he does, the best way to really understand history is to live in the wilderness."

"Right," Scott said, tone dipped in sarcasm. "Bet we find flat screens, sailboats, and a **Über** estate."

"Sam isn't like that," Beth defended. "He's very much in tune with nature." Then she paused and realized her "tense" was incorrect. "I guess, I meant he *was* in tune with nature."

Scott reached over and touched her hand sympathetically. He knew the pain of lost, especially without warning; the emptiness you feel inside due to missing that person. The hole it leaves in the core of your essence. Sam was not only her teacher, but he was also a close friend and confidant.

The couple finally made it to the house; and just like Scott suspected it was a nice looking estate in the middle of a Floridian forest. Scott carried three large bags while Beth took in her small purse and book bag into the house. The evening air smelled fresh and smooth. The birds sang and the crickets chirped into the crescent mooned night.

When Beth open the door Scott noticed the large plasma TV in the living room, "What did I tell you: flat screens."

Beth cut her eyes at Scott before dropping her bags at the door. Beth walked the across the sprawling three bedroom Victorian styled home. Scott looked through the fridge for a beer; luckily there was a remaining Corona.

Beth walked to the study. Beth could feel something watching her but assumed it was just nerves, regardless her stomach dipped and spun the closer she got to the study.

She cried out. Scott put down the Corona he found and ran up the stairs calling her name. He found Beth in the doorway of the study staring down at a dried puddle of blood. The crusted blood had caked on the soft white carpet that covered the study's floor. Horrified Beth froze; never in her life had she seen so much blood. Then it dawned on her that instance, that was the very spot where Sam took his last breath.

The look on Beth's face was familiar to Scott. It was the same look he gave when he killed his first insurgent. The horror that reflected in her blue eyes mirrored the horror that he saw six years ago. Scott walked over to her, placing his strong hand on her shoulder. "Do you want to go?" he asks.

"No," she said meekly, allowing one lone tear to collect in her left eye, "we have to find it."

"What exactly is '*it*' anyhow?"

Beth lounged over the blood, feeling it would be disrespectful to step in the blood of her mentor. "Sam told me he found something that was very special while we were at Flinders' Island. He said it was an Aborigines urn."

Scott watched Beth ramble frantically through Sam's drawers. He was concerned about her true intentions. "We aren't stealing things are we?"

Beth met his eyes with a disappointed gaze, "How do you think I got the key?"

Silenced, Scott looked away as Beth continued her hunt. Scott felt wrong; in his mind they were violating Sam's home by searching through the dead man's belongings. But Scott went along with it because ultimately his faith lied in Beth. Scott stared deep into the stain; he turns his head in disgust.

In the corner of his eyes he sees a brown clay jar. Creeping to the corner near the bookshelf Scott examined the jar from a far. Scott crotched down to get a closer look; the jar looked ancient, covered in unintelligible glyphs. The lid was beside the jar along with dust and what appeared to be bone fragments.

"I think I found something Beth," Scott as he picked up the jar and it's lid.

"DON'T TOUCH ANYTHING WITH YOUR HAND!" Beth exclaimed running over to Scott. Beth knew artifacts were not only precious but extremely fragile.

Taken aback by the scolding Scott passed the jar to Beth. "Sorry – I didn't know."

Realizing how harsh she sounded, Beth apologized to her lover. She held the jar that was remarkable durable, shockingly for something that appeared to be very old. She examined the jar closer attempting to read the glyphs but had difficulties in translation.

"There's like bones and stuff right here" Scott said pointing to the pile of remains.

Beth carefully looked at the bone fragments; without carbon dating she could only estimate the urn was of Palawan decent. The Palawans were the indigenous people of Tasmania before the European settler introduced disease and exterminated the Palawans.

Beth was familiar with the history of the Palawan people, but judging from the age of this urn; this was the oldest artifact from the Palawan she has ever seen. She was unsure of the burial rituals of this lost people but whatever it was had her attention.

"Sam must have some text –"

A blur sped past Beth and that blur formed into a man, and that man had Scott by throat pinning him tightly to the wall. He stood strong, dark olive skin, lose curls, and a daggered mouth. Scott's mouth gaped open from the shock of lying eyes on Aryk once more.

How could he find me, Scott thought. Aryk's face was in a hissing frown; his ivory fangs protrude over his soft lips. Aryk's eyes shown bright sea green. The anger of the vampire was painted over his face. His angelic features were ferocious and craved destruction.

"Why are you here –" Aryk asked through a growl still chocking the life from Scott's body. Before Scott had a chance to think, let alone lie Aryk threatened "– I will rip out your larynx!"

Scott could not speak, his throat was being crushed. His breathing was completed compromised and he was beginning to pass out. Beth cried out for the vampire to let Scott go, but her please were ignored. Aryk wanted to know how the mortal found him. His memory was supposed to be cleared; he had ceased all connections with Scott. How did his human find this place and how did he know Aryk would be in this place.

"I – I – can't…" Scott gargled desperately attempting to speak.

"You wish to *destroy* me?" Aryk asked rhetorically. "It can't be done – understand me. I am immortal!"

"Let him go, we don't know you, please," Beth begged through tears.

Aryk paused, he heard the pleas of the girl, and retracted his fangs and loosened his grip on Scott allowing him to slide to the floor. Scott's eyes had rolled to the back of his head from almost fainting from his lack of air. Aryk was not sympathetic, he simply wanted answers. And killing everyone in the room would not yield those answers.

"Ok, Scott, explain?" Aryk said folding his arms.

"Who are you?" Beth asked.

Aryk cut his eyes at the girl, "*I'm* the interviewee here." Aryk returned his gaze to Scott who was beginning to regain consciousness. "Scott, explain."

Hoarse and out of breath Scott said, "This, this is Beth's boss' home."

"Bullshit." Aryk was not buying it. Aryk was sure it was some type of locator spell, mortals were known for using magic against vampires.

"It's true," Scott protested. "Her boss, Sam, was killed by some kind of animal; we are just here to pick up a few things, I swear. I had no idea – I didn't even know you were – I thought I was going crazy." Scott began to rant as he attempted in vain to get his breathing pattern corrected.

Folding his arms and shifting his hips in suspicion Aryk asked, "So you being here is some type of coincidence."

"Or fate," Scott responded.

Aryk could not help but smile, it was too delicious. The thought of this reunion just being a coincidence was hilarious even so Aryk had to smile. His eyes cut to Beth who held onto the ancient jar for dear life.

"What do you have there, dear?"

She held the jar closer to her heart fearfully. Aryk began to stalk Beth who began to cower into the study's corner. Smiling darkly, Aryk watched Beth fear reach her eyes. "I will only ask once, cupcake. After that people start bleeding."

The air was cut by the speed of a blade and that blade cut through Aryk's skull. The vampire was brought his knees and as quickly as Aryk fell, a large onyx skinned man held him up by his throat. The dark figures hair was as sable as his skin but his hair was a soft as silk.

Red paint was scribbled across his muscled ink colored frame. His eyes were dark and lifeless. He lifted Aryk off the floor and tossed the vampire across the room.

Something reacted in Scott; the urge to defend Aryk rose from his blood. Scott quickly pulled out his silver nine millimeter and fired four shots into the man's chest. The man surprised by the heat of the bullets, paused for a second. Scott attempted to fire again but the man using a thrust from his palm sent Scott through the thin plaster wall.

The man then placed his gaze on Beth. He began to shout in an unintelligible tongue. But Beth had an idea of what he wanted. He wanted the urn; however Beth resisted. Angered the man tossed the large desk that separated him from Beth across the room.

"I did not appreciate that," Aryk said, now standing right next to the man. Aryk was completed healed, and fuming. The vampire grabbed the Tribal Man by the throat and slammed him angrily to the floorboards. The vampire pinned the Tribal Man to the ground and delivered a barrage of fist to his face. The Tribal Man reversed the hold rolling out of the vampire's grip.

Both monsters were to their feet. The Tribal Man's hands began to tremble and morphed from humanoid hands, to claw like talons. Aryk was unsure what he was fighting, but he was about to play in its entrails for his sneak attack.

Aryk using his blurring vampire speed pounced but was caught by the sharp claws of the Tribal Man. The Tribal Man, still using the vampire's momentum threw Aryk down the stairs of the large home.

Tribal Man placed his gaze back on Beth again. Fear pumped violently though her body; Tribal Man could sense it. He then morphed into his true form; a midsized dog like beast, a dark brown color with sixteen tan trips on its lower back. The sight shocked and frightened her so greatly that she dropped the urn. The urn rolled over to the beast that picked it up with his mouth, and with its swift speed leapt out of the window into the night.

She recognized the animal; it was an animal that she was sure was extinct. It was the thylacine, a carnivorous marsupial from Tasmania. She was sure they were all gone due to European introduction to the continent, but even if they were not extinct, she was sure they were not supposed to shape shift.

Aryk had regained consciousness and he was even more upset than he was before. Speeding up the winding stairs he saw Beth crying. *What is she crying for*, he thought, *the thing didn't even touch her*. Then the question of why was she spared entered his mind.

Aryk reached down pulling a crying Beth to her feet. "Why were you spared? What was that thing? Why did it want that jar?"

"I don't know," she cried. "Please, I don't know."

"Aryk," Scott called out.

Aryk heard his offspring-to-be crying out for help. Aryk dropped Beth and walked over to Scott who was collecting himself; his face was dusted with plaster and covered with small scratches on his cheek. Aryk was already healed and Scott, now a vampire-human hybrid, had slowly began to recover also.

"I'm going to require answers."

Aryk drove the pickup truck back to his Rosewood estate. Beth held a tome she took from Sam's study. Scott sat in the front with Aryk but no one spoke. When Aryk made it to his hidden mansion he could sense his guest.

Mika stood in the doorway, holding a martini glass full of blood from a Thai virgin; a particular favorite of Aryk. Mika could sense humans approaching; she got aroused at the idea that she and Aryk would have a bloody orgy like they did in the thirties.

"Those were the days," Mika said, reminiscing to herself.

Angelique watched the approaching car from a window in the hallway. She watched Aryk climb out the truck with two humans. Though she lacked mystical powers, she could tell by the apparent terror on their faces that they are human.

"So, are *they* for dinner?" Mika asked, exposing her sharp fangs.

"I was attacked," Aryk said, "by some type of Thylacine – shape-shifting creature."

"*What*?" Mika asked, astonished.

Beth saw it as her time to chime in, "Thylacines are extinct marsupials from –"

"Duh, I know what they are. They were hideous little fuckers; glad they're gone." Mika gave Beth a glare then focused on Aryk, "You give them permission to talk?"

"Play nice," Aryk said to Mika.

Aryk then led Scott and Beth into his home. Both were shocked at Aryk's home. From the outside it looked like a semi worn-out Victorian home; but the inside was deck out with blush furniture and state of the art appliances.

Aryk explained to Mika what he experienced hours before. Mika, being an elder vampire was trained in the supernatural and was familiar with many different beings that existed in that plane of existence.

"Sounds like you are dealing with a Sleether," Mika said, sipping her blood martini. "Often time demons take the form of animals to hide their existence. It's easier to blend in that way, but it's rare that you come across a Sleether since they are extinct."

"So is the Thylacine," Scott added. "Guess it didn't get the message that it's extinct."

Mika could sense Aryk inside of Scott, Aryk had shared his essence through The Bite with Scott. Any mortal who is still alive after The Bite is usually turned into a vampire. "Well I haven't heard of a Sleether in almost two hundred years. The last one was slew in Africa by a band of mortals. They don't procreate like your normal demon; they need to be conjured into existence. They require a talisman, magic lamp, something to hold its essence"

"The urn," Beth said.

"I guess," Mika said.

"The urn had bones and fragments inside," Aryk said. "Perhaps when the urn was opened the essence of the demon was released into the ether."

"I'm not following," Scott said. All the metaphysical rubbish was confusing him.

"You don't need to," Aryk said. "How do I kill this *Sleether?*"

"Well I would start with the urn," Mika said. "It is the Sleether's only link to its power. Otherwise, it's indestructible. I'm sure it had to have fed off humans, otherwise it would be no stronger than the animal it manifested itself as."

Aryk grinned, he underestimated the Sleether but he had no intentions on doing that again. Aryk had the heart of a warrior, so the idea of the impending battle excited him heavily. "Fine, it can't be too far."

"Wait," Mika said with a small grin. "If you think this will be an easy task you are insane, Aryk. Sleether's are remarkably strong, especially after they have fed on human flesh. You will require backup."

"Concerned are we?" Aryk said with a grin.

"Not really, I just have no interest in babysitting your mortals."

"Fair enough." Aryk walked over to his closet and opened it. In the closet Aryk had a large number, ancient and modern weaponry. Aryk removed a late medieval long-sword. The handle was iron with gold accents and its blade was long but somewhat thin. Aryk loved these but rarely got a chance to use one. He felt like King Arthur every time he held it. A smile burned through his lips.

"I'm going with you," Scott declared reaching for a sword but was stopped by Aryk.

"Do you even know how to use this?" Scott gave Aryk no reply. Aryk smiled before digging in a small drawer and removed a Desert Eagle. "Bet you know how this works."

"Damn straight," Scott confirmed.

"Don't get too excited boys," Mika said.

"Angelique, keep our guest comfortable," Aryk commanded. Armed with his weapon Aryk walked to his porch.

Scott trailed behind Aryk and Mika. Mika watched Aryk sniff rapidly searching for the Sleether. Aryk found the trail and a dark smile appeared but then evaporated. Aryk extended his hand to Scott. "Take my hand, we're flying."

Scott hesitated but Aryk spoke in a soft tone, "You were born for this, Scott." Scott reluctantly took Aryk's cold clammy hand. Aryk pulled Scott closer to him. "Hold on tight."

With lightening speed the two vampires and one hybrid took off into the night's sky. They rocketed into the clouds but Scott could not see, he would not allow himself to see. He pressed his face into Aryk's chest trying his best to imagine he was on a rollercoaster. Aryk's speed was like no vehicle Scott had ever been in; now imbued with enhanced human strength, Scott could hold on to the wild bronco that was Aryk.

Aryk's vampire eyes could see into the dark as if it was day. Aryk sense of smell picked up the odor of the Sleether making Aryk grinned with anticipation. Aryk was about to bring the pain.

Chapter

9

Beth sat nervously next to Angelique who watched Beth closely. Beth would not be so uncomfortable if Angelique was not holding a shotgun. Angelique was not happy this bitch was here, in her home. Angelique was not in the loop and that was not acceptable.

For years Angelique and Aryk shared a soul; her life was his only link back to his humanity. The bound between Aryk and Angelique was stronger than blood and bone; so why were these strangers more involved than she?

Angelique was at war within; she wanted to quiz Beth about what was happening. But she feared that would give her even more of the upper-hand. She could not have that shit. But she was not a fool. Angelique knew the question that bounced in her blonde head were more powerful than any buckshot.

"Who the *fuck* are you?" Angelique asked.

Taken back by Angelique's rudeness, but more concerned what the gun wielding woman would do next. "I'm Beth, I'm Scott's fiancé."

"What happen earlier," her voice hallow. Angelique leaned in closer to Beth. She wanted to look into Beth's fearful eyes. Angelique's was gaze terrifyingly beautiful; her hazel eyes suck her in with a vortex's ferocity. Initially Beth sat quietly, almost too shaken to speak. A smile burned through Angelique ruby lips as she cocked her shot gun.

"Don't play with *me*, bitch."

A storm cloud of terror rocked Beth's chest, "We were going to my boss's house." Beth broke into small sobs and guilt filled Angelique's heart. Realizing that she earnestly hurt the young lady Angelique decided another approach.

"It's scary isn't it?" Angelique asked as Beth continued to meekly sob. Angelique hands her a small tissue, "How did it all start?"

Beth explained how she worked as an intern for an Archeologist; she told Angelique about how her boss was killed by some wild animal. Beth explained to her about how the Tribal Man appeared right after Aryk and stole the urn from them. She never says anything about the connection between Scott and Aryk.

Did not matter though; Angelique understood better than even Scott, Aryk intentions.

Angelique was fascinated by how Beth managed to be a part of game. Aryk made it clear nights before that he wished to turn Scott into vampire but she wasn't sure how Beth played into that plan. Would turn Beth as well –a gift that he denied Angelique for many years.

"You do know what is going on, right."

"No fucking clue," Beth confessed. "I have no idea how – I just want to go home."

"But you know what *they* are," Angelique quizzed. She really wanted to know exactly how much Beth comprehended.

"Demons," Beth answered. "Monsters."

"Vampires," Angelique answered.

Beth's mind had not yet gripped the reality of the situation; her common sense wared with what she learned on this night. "Vampires –"

"– Among other things are real."

"How?"

Angelique rose and dropped her shoulders. "We have no complete understanding of the world we live in. Vampires are a part of this world."

"Are there many?"

"No," Angelique decided to inform Beth more. "To my understanding there are only a few in existences. Being a vampire is not a simple thing to be these days."

Beth accepted that answer; after seeing shape-shifting marsupials and people flying, vampires seemed to be a very feasible answer. "Are you a vampire?"

"No." Angelique's tone seemed as if she wanted nothing else to do with Beth.

Beth however had more question. She wanted to know how long they would be held hostage. She wanted to know how Aryk knew her fiancé. She wanted answers. But Angelique kept quiet; she felt it was her duty to protect Aryk at all cost.

"Answer me, God damn you," she exclaimed desperately.

Angelique gave her a dark smile, "You want the *God damn* truth?" Silence. "What do you drink?"

"Not blood."

Angelique smiled as she walked into the kitchen, there she retrieved a bottle of Skyy Vodka and poured it into two small glasses. "Your fiancé has been chosen, Aryk wants him to be his partner."

"*Excuse me!*" Beth squealed. "Scott is not gay."

"Vampire's do not think like me and you," Angelique clarified. "Vampires, when they get to a certain age they require another immortal for company. Aryk is no different; he found your Scott and he feels that he would be the most appropriate for his partner. He's most likely going to turn him tonight."

It dawned on Beth what was happening. She was separated from Scott and now Aryk would complete his evil plan of turning her Scott into a monster; into a vampire. With one quick chug Beth completed her drink. "I'm going to need another one of those."

"You've fucked with the wrong vampire, sleether" Aryk declared to the Tribal Man who had a small camp fire roaring. In one hand he held the urn and the other an arm of one of his victims. Aryk could smell burning flesh before he landed in the wooded swamp. But Aryk noticed what was going on; the urn, the burning human flesh, the dripping human arm. It was ritual.

Vampires are highly sensitive to magic; Mika remained many feet away from Aryk and the Sleether. Scott however stayed right on Aryk's heels; with a flip of Aryk's wrist Scott began to ease off. Aryk's pride and arrogance made him want to face the Sleether alone.

"Aryk, he's using magic," Mika warned Aryk. Vampires are highly susceptible to magic; even a vampire like Aryk could be taken by a well casted spell.

Aryk already knew there was a high probability of magic being used in their battle but Aryk has survived magical assaults before. Aryk was seasoned, even though he has not encountered a Sleether before this night. He was sure it could not be too difficult to kill.

It was not just Aryk pride that made him decline Scott's assistance. Aryk was unsure how powerful his foe truly was. The last time the vampire encountered the Tribal Man he was easily over powered. This was strange for a vampire who recently fed; after Dead Things feed they are at their most powerful. Aryk knew that magic could affect Mika. She was just as powerfully as him. But Scott still being mostly human would have a better chance at evading a magical attack.

The Sleether spoke in his Aborigines language. The grunts were low and shallow, Aryk, though a multi-linguist was unfamiliar with the language. His voice was hypnotic and pace; Aryk braced himself for an attack, but realized the words lack the flow of an incantation.

Aryk's body tensed, and the Sleether could tell. He could sense the vampire anxiety, a smile burned through his dark face. Aryk was getting agitated by the Tribal Man's nonsensical language. Aryk lifted his sword ready to strike before he was stopped in his track. The Sleether extended his hand, and in a boisterous voice he cried out, "**Makara!**"

Magic! Roared in Aryk's Mind. *Magic, I knew it would be magic.*

Aryk's attack was frozen by the Sleether's magics; the magic held the vampire in its tar-like force. Aryk however did not resist; Aryk did not sense malevolence behind the magic that was used. Aryk sought an understanding. Terror raised in Scott; pumping lava roughly through his veins.

Scott pointed his gun at the Sleether threateningly but Mika stopped his attack

"Let him," he demanded. "Aryk is in no danger." She knew how proud Aryk was, she wanted Aryk to handle it *his* way.

Scott never moved his gun; screw what this crazy bitch was talking about. Scott may not have fired but he had no intentions of removing his crosshairs off the Tribal Man. He had power; so much power that he render a vampire as powerful as Aryk to a submissive victim. Scott would not take any chances.

The Sleether completed his bewitchment. *Now, hear me in your mind,* the Sleether's voice echoed in Aryk consciousness. The Sleether completed his psychic link with Aryk. The link was easy to form with Aryk being a willing participant.

Telepathy? Aryk spoke through his mind but it was still peppered with sarcasm. *So juvenile.*

It was the only way I could reach you. The Sleether responded.

Aryk could sense that the being was young. The Tribal Man's mind seemed fresh but old at the same time; it was as a youth from the past found its way to the future. It's mind was clouded with old customs and since extinct philosophies. But this was good to know, because Aryk would not have to fear the Tribal Man magical abilities. Telepathy is one of the lowest forms of magic.

As much as Aryk was rambling through the mind of his foe, the Tribal Man also searched through Aryk's mind. But vampires often try to read other vampires minds; thus Aryk and older vampires like him usually build psychic blocks in their minds. Aryk could sense the Tribal Man's attempt to discover his secrets.

Our talk is the same now, The Sleether said to Aryk telepathically.

Fine then, Aryk responded. *Talk to me.*

We wish to take our land back!

You are mistaken, Aryk responded – his tone blunt and forthright. *This isn't Australia.*

We existed before blood beast like you had form in this dimension!

This world was never yours, Aryk countered. *You have no claim on it.*

It was stolen; like all things in this new world. A stolen land that was built up by stolen people —yet you *defend it.*

What are you called? Aryk diverted. Aryk could sense the Sleether thinking – he did not understand the vampire. *Do you have a name?*

Scott did not like what he saw, Aryk was all but kneeling, and his arms were extended like a crane. The Sleether had all the control. He could simply kill Aryk with a simple strike and then kill both himself and Mika. Scott knew once he fed off of his human flesh he would be even stronger.

"Mika, we gotta do something," Scott said.

"I am," Mika said as she slid her hand into her pocket. She retrieved a small velvet bag; she poured the contents into her hand. Vampires may be weak against magics but they too have their own rituals that can disable magic. She brought her right hand to her mouth and with a blow she hissed *"Perturbare!"*

The link that glued the Sleether to Aryk was destroyed. Mika used anti-magic to release Aryk from the grips of the Sleether. The separation was so quick Aryk was unsure if his last telepathic message was delivered.

No matter, Aryk knew all he needed to about the Sleether. Aryk, now freed from the bewitchment raises his sword to strike but the Sleether spoke, "**MARRA!**"

The night winds picked up; the airstream violently assaulted the vampires and hybrid but the Sleether stood still. *More magic he thought;* Aryk's only option was to attack before it was too late. Aryk wobbly attempted to stand as the harsh storm wiped mercilessly against his cold dead skin.

The Tribal Man held the bleeding arm over the urn, small drops of blood fell inside the urn. A flash of light appeared blinding all anti-heroes. Scott skin warmed from the incandescent flare; it was intense and visually offensive, but Scott could not turn away. Scott knew he needed to brace himself for whatever came next.

The wind began to decrease. The spell's power had reached its climax. When the blinding flash subsided another Sleether appeared in its Thylacine form. *Another one,* Aryk thought as he angled his blade to fight. Taken by surprise, the new Sleether pounces Aryk. Again the original Sleether, the Tribal Man, screamed out, "**MARRA!**" and with a flash of incandescent brilliance another appeared.

Attempting to get an upper-hand Mika threw two small steel darts at the urn. She realized that as long as the urn was not broken, more sleethers could be conjured. One step ahead of her the Tribal Man turned away from the assault, opting to take the shards in his back instead. Facing away the Tribal Man conjured another and another. Aryk penetrated his blade through the chest of the first Sleether but then realized there were more.

The Tribal Man had created more demonic-thylacine and though Aryk slew many of them he could sense the battle would eventually get out of control. A group of Sleether attempted to overwhelm Mika; but her fighting skills could not be reckoned with. The ancient vampire used her bare hands to kill numerous infant Sleethers.

Bullet sounds rang out into the night. Scott used great precision when he fired his gun. He only aimed for the head; blowing the enemy skulls to pieces. His marksmanship skills were impeccable but he would run out of bullets soon. The futility of their situation was apparent.

"We have to retreat," Scott announces as he fired another bullet into the brain of an approaching Sleether.

Aryk knew this already – he just needed a small diversion. "Do you have another grenade?" The amount of Sleethers had grown beyond what the Aryk could vanquish.

"Couldn't get it on the plane." Scott confessed.

Backing away from the small growing army of Sleethers – Aryk, Mika, and Scott took off into the forest. Aryk could sense the terror rise in Scott's blood. *Run,* Aryk commanded. But Aryk refused to leave the battle; like a cub to it mother, Scott refused to leave as well.

"I will catch up with you," Aryk promised. "You need to run, now. You won't make much of a vampire if you are dead."

Scott ran blindly into the darkness of Floridian woods. Aryk and Mika rocketed to the sky out of the reach of all Sleethers. The Tribal Man did not appreciate this act of cowardice and had no intentions on letting the vampires escape.

With his enhanced hearing Scott could hear two sleethers chasing him into the forest. Scott could feel them approaching; his heart raced wildly as sound of their paws their got louder and louder. They were coming for him; Scott knew he could not fight them in the dark, but he could run no further. Turning around, standing his ground he raised his weapon and fired into the darkness.

While firing into the dark Scott was lifted into the air by Aryk.

Chapter

<u>10</u>

Beth was startled when she heard large thuds sounds outside the large house. Grabbing the shotgun, Angelique walked over to the door, but Aryk and company barged in forcefully. Angelique noticed the dirt in Aryk's hair; knowing Aryk is meticulous about his hair, she knew the shit had hit the fan. "What happened?"

Aryk did not say a syllable to Angelique while entering – his mind was too busy to explain anything to her. He organized his thoughts and began to formulate a plan. It is not unheard of for other demons to challenge vampires, but it is not something that is commonplace occurrences.

"We need weapons," Aryk affirmed.

"Oh shit," Angelique said – she knew this was not good. Aryk never panic; all this time Angelique thought Aryk was built without fear.

Panicking Beth asked. "What's happening?"

"You're most likely going to be eviscerated," Mika said with a girlish sweetness. "But you didn't hear that from me."

"You know the monster that tried to kill us at Sam's –" Scott began to explained before being cut off by Mika.

"– The Sleether has multiplied and is coming to kill all the humans."

"What?" Angelique said eyes wide and horrified.

"How do you know they are coming here?" Scott asked Mika.

"They need human flesh," Mika said.

"And this house separates them from Sumner – a town full of humans," Aryk said looking out his window, waiting desperately for the Sleethers to show themselves.

"If you want to kill them, this stage would be the easiest," Mika said. "Once they feed on live human flesh they will be as indestructible as the first one."

"He uses magics," Aryk said eyes still glued to the forest. "Angelique, pull the magical text, Mika watch the girl, Scott come with me."

Aryk lead his progeny-to-be back to the weapons closet. Aryk opened the two-door closet displaying numerous weapons that were in the lit cherry wood closet. Aryk flip a light switch within the closet; the switch opened an additional compartment where automatic weaponry was present.

Aryk passed Scott a dual automatic rifle, "Are you familiar with this gun, it's Peruvian."

"Got the ammo?"

Aryk smiled at Scott gusto, "I want to show you something else."

Through the kitchen and down the stairs Aryk lea Scott to his basement, And like much of the multimillion dollar estate it was too redone. The once dark, dank basement was replaced with a gym. Mirrors lined the walls along with weapons that varied and time period and origin.

"I guess you work out a lot." Scott could not help but notice the mirrors and that Aryk's image could be seen in them. *That answers that myth.*

"It never hurts to expand on what you already know." Aryk walked over the wall that was covered with mirrors. Aryk slides one mirror to the left then pressed a small button hidden behind the mirror. You could hear the motor hiss as a small compartment rolled out a small wooden coffin.

"You actually sleep in caskets?"

Aryk cut his sea colored eyes at Scott – "No." as the casket rolled itself complete out of its holding area.

Aryk spoke in a monotone voice, "Well before I was made, vampires would hide in coffins to escape human hunters and sunlight. With the future bringing newer threats I have enhanced the capabilities of the coffin. If I am wounded heavily I need to be placed into my coffin until I heal. I cannot risk being found by other vampires."

"Why are you giving me this responsibility," Scott asked suspiciously. "Why not tell Angelique or Mika?"

"Because, I have chosen you," Aryk said. Looking aimlessly into the coffin Aryk confessed, "There are many secrets that I have never shared with anyone, not even Angelique. More than her *you* share my soul. When I chose you I chose you because you are strong –strong enough to stand side by side with me. A great honor has been bestowed upon you."

"You're wrong," Scott protested. "I'm not –"

"– A killer?" Aryk cut him off and broke his own gaze. "You are. You left the mortal coil a long time ago. You knew where this was leading. Accept your gift – assuming you survive."

"Why are you telling me this," Scott's voice was dripped in suspicion.

The hairs on Aryk's body stood up. He could sense them approaching. "They are here."

Beth read the magical text that Angelique brought from Aryk's private library, there were only three books and they did not look as old as she imagined magic books to be. The books were bound by leather but appeared to be no older than twenty years.

"What are we supposed to do with these?" Beth asked.

"Use them if necessary," Mika stated coldly. "I'm not sure exactly how much magic this Sleether has but I do not plan on getting hypnotized like Aryk did."

"Vampires are very weak against magic," Angelique said.

Mika cut her eyes at Angelique angered that she would release such sensitive information to Beth. Beth saw the look; unsure of the complete powers of vampires Beth kept it herself. "What kind of magic trick are we using?"

"*Magic trick?*" Mika echoed in a nasally tone.

"A biding spell could keep them at least in this area, so they can't get to Sumner," Angelique stated. "I'm no witch but I can perform this with assistance."

"Just make sure you know what you're doing. I am not trying to be turned into a warthog," Mika cut her eyes and went to find Aryk.

Beth read the pages and noticed that most of the incantation looked like Latin. Beth only took one year of Latin and only got a basic understanding of the long dead language. Beth rummaged through the book desperately for something she could use in the future.

Aryk made his way up the stairs with weapons in his possession. Mika needed to speak to Aryk but only wanted Aryk to hear her. Of all the languages that both he and she knew, she chose Haitian Creole. She asked Aryk, "lèzòm plan an yo sèvi ak majik Pyèj kont

Sleether." *(They plan to use binding magic against the Sleether.)*

Aryk smiled; rarely does he get a chance to use this language. "Bon, n ap kanpe gad deyò. Pa gen anyen vin sot pase nou." *(Good, we will guard the outside. Nothing can pass us.)*

Beth ears began to burn, as she is familiar with Haitian Creole. She listened in closely to Mika.

"Mwen pa renmen blond a (*I don't like the blonde*)," Mika said with a snarl. "Nou pral touye l 'anvan oswa apre? (*Will we kill her before or after*)"

"After," Aryk said in plain English. But Aryk warned, "Ti gason an pa apa nan jwèt sa (*the boy is not a part of this game*)." Aryk then shifted his eyes to Scott, "He's going to be hungry."

"Li konnen ou manje sou, sè l ' (*Does he know that you fed on his sister*)?"

Aryk quickly shifted his head to meet Mika's. Anger had risen in his blood and it was visible in his eyes. "Watch your mouth," he warned.

"You are playing a dangerous game," Mika concluded. "Just make sure my fangs won't get broken all for the sake of your *game*."

A cry of the wild echoed through the night, it was a loud wail that everyone in the estate could hear clearly. "It's time. Start the spell; I'm sure they will try to run around us so work fast. If they get past us bullets will kill these creatures. Mika, Scott, we have work to do."

Armed with their weapons the warriors matched to the front lawn. Mika held a spike mace, Aryk wielding his knight's long-sword, and Scott with his automatic weapon. The vampires stood still as statues; they tuned into nature using their entire bodies to hear their enemies. Scott sweated profusely with anticipation.

Anxiety rose in Scott's blood; he could taste it. He was familiar with this feeling; he experienced it every day while in Iraq. Scott's was an excellent soldier, but due to his current medications, he had lost his patience and poise. "How many do you think there are?" he finally asked – but it received no reply. Scott continued to rattle on about how nervous and afraid he was.

"Fucking mortals," Mika hissed under her breath.

Scott's back pocket vibrated and Nicki Minaj's "Super Bass" played; Mika looked over at the human before chuckling. "It's Beth," Scott defended. Scott took out his phone and read the damning text message:

They're going to kill us after this. Aryk Killed Cecil. If we make it we have to get out of here.

"Get your head in the game!" Aryk screamed at his pupil. The thud of the incoming stampede of thylacine could be heard. "It's starting."

Chapter

<u>11</u>

Beth watched Angelique set up the magical circle; Beth did not trust Angelique just as she did not trust Aryk. She needed to find a trump card; she refused to die here. Not this day. But two things were trying to kill her; an army of thylacine and vampires, both she thought did not exist three hours ago.

"We must bless the circle," Angelique said. "Sit with me, Indian style."

Beth entered the circle that was surrounded by sea salt. The center was a Black Mirror, used for conjuring spirits. Each point of the rhombus mirror had a white candle. Next to the mirror sat a small dagger. Angelique remembers the small chant and began to murmur in Latin the incantation, "*Ligare, ligare, ligare.*"

Beth looked frantically through the magical text; she needed to find something she could use to defend herself with. As the battle raged on and Angelique cast her spell beside her; Beth found exactly what she needed.

Aryk caught the first beast with his sword. Another beast appeared and with a mighty swing the vampire be-headed the monster. A third stalked Aryk from the corner; but the vampire was too powerful, too wise to be taken by surprise. With a huge thrust, Aryk penetrated the brain of the monster.

Mika swung her mace, bashing in the faces and bodies of each Sleether that she encountered. But the show-off in Mika made her go the extra mile. Mike leapt in the air swinging her spiked weapon crushing the faces of her foes.

She would blow kisses, tumble, and do the splits to show how simple it was to defeat her opponents. Who would notice such a thing? Not Aryk; he was too busy looking for the lead Sleether and Scott was barely hanging on to life. No, Mika loved to entertain herself, more than anything.

Scott was bushwhacked by the text he received but he had to fight. He was back in the battlefield and like in Iraq; all personal issues must be settle after the battle. So Cecil was banished from his mind –for the time being.

Thylacine, sensing the human flesh attempted to overwhelm Scott, but his marksmanship had no trouble navigating bullets through their head.

Scott senses now enhanced, could see his enemies no matter how cloaked by shadows they were. But the Sleether often bypassed the vampire and ran directly for the human. Mika noticed this before Aryk who desperately searched for the Tribal Man.

A Sleether crept behind Scott who was occupied firing bullets at his assailants. Mika knew that if that creature fed off Scott, they would have a bigger problem. With very few options, Mika hurled her mace that the creature. The powerful weapon collided with creatures face, killing it instantly.

"Watch your ass," Mika yelled out.

Two Sleether passed the blockade created by Aryk and entered the house. The two beasts could smell two different humans in the home. Angelique continued to chant as the beast entered the home. The first beast was met by Aryk's white Siberian Husky, Lou who pounced the Thylacine biting deep into its throat. Beth retrieved the shotgun next to Angelique and fired once, miss. Twice, miss. She pumped again and as the beast attempted to pounce her she fired a shot into its ribs killing the creature.

Angelique could feel the magics course through her; the power was orgasmic and almost overtook her. Angelique rode the mystical rollercoaster, retaining her composure. Angelique picked up the dagger and cut into the palm of her hand, dropping the blood onto the black mirror.

Using her will she bound the Thylacine to this area. Another Sleether breached the home; Beth attempted to fire again, click. The weapon was out of ammo. The Sleether mouth held the urn; that's when the blonder realized who he was. the Sleether dropped the urn morphed into the Tribal Man –nude covered in his aborigines glyphs.

"That's him," Beth whispered to Angelique. "I'm out of shells. Do you have a plan?"

"I'm going to charge him," Angelique said. "Run up stairs; Aryk house is basically an arsenal."

"It won't matter, he will just chase me," Beth stated. "Nowhere to run."

Accepting their situation Angelique gave her a trusting nod. Holding the dagger Angelique charged the Tribal Man and with one strong thrust Angelique was repelled away from the fight. Beth swung the shot gun like a mallet and collided with the Sleether's back. The Sleether turned with a growl prepared to strike. Before the beast could attack Lou, Aryk's brave Husky, pounced the beast in Beth's defense. But the Sleether was too fast to be caught by a dog.

"Put down my dog," Aryk demanded.

The Tribal Man grinned, his teeth covered in dark taffy like grime. Aryk noted that this was the first display of human like emotions from the Sleether. He began to rant in his language, but Aryk did not understand nor did he care to understand. Aryk had very little patience for non-Latin based languages

"I don't care about any of that," Aryk said in a low hoarse growl. "Put down my *dog!*"

The Sleether could sense Aryk's tension and the fact that Aryk cared for the animal. A dark grin appeared on the Tribal Man's face. The Sleether attempted to break the animal's neck but Aryk's vampiric speed compounded when his rage was released. With blurring speed Aryk punched the Tribal Man out, knocking him across the room and releasing his animal.

Aryk kneeled down to check on his pet, Lou had scratches and the dog's soft fur was covered slightly with blood. "Louise, you are a very brave girl. Go to my room." The animal, well trained limped up to the Aryk's room.

The Tribal Man was shocked by the vampire's strength, but was prepared to do battle with Aryk. "There are few things that I simply don't tolerate: upsetting my house, fucking with my hair, and my pooch. And you managed to do all four all in the same night."

The Sleether face began to morph monstrously, his face began to bulge and stretch violently. Aryk watched as the Sleether's mouth expanded, his teeth sharpened, his eyes went a soulless black. His nails sharpen like animal claws. Aryk was waiting for this, for him to show his true colors.

"Nice teeth, want to see mine," Aryk dared, the vampire quickly exposed his fangs.

Scott began to panic; he ran out of ammo and Mika was running out of endurance. A large Sleether leapt into the air lead by his claws and fangs. Scott quickly swung his FAD, knocking the Thylacine down.

Scott ran over to the mace, once wielded by Mika. Scott used all his strength to bash in the brains of the Sleether.

"There are too many," Scott declared. Scott's endurance fading and a open cut began to drain the energy out of him. "I don't know what to – it's just too many."

Mika scanned the yard; eleven Sleethers were left. "Hmmm..." Mika then looked over to Scott and gave him a naughty wink. "Good luck!" Mika then rocketed into the sky, leaving Scott to fend for himself.

"Fucking, bitch!" Scott screamed out. The Sleethers began to prowl the hybird backing Scott to the porch. Scott could hear the low growls of the monsters and the hair stood erect on his necks.

Scott had to retreat. With no back up Scott ran into the house and closed the large wooden door. His vision was blurred due to the cut on his forehead mixing with sweating and getting into his eyes. With no other ideas Scott placed his back against the door and hope that he could keep them out.

Scott turned to the living room where he saw Aryk and the Tribal Man's battle. Scott wanted to help Aryk but he could not move his body. Scott could feel the outside Sleethers clawing at the door angrily. Scott looked around the room for something that he could use to prop the door close.

Aryk fought intensely with the Tribal Man. Aryk's strength dwarfed in comparison to the Sleether. The Sleether lifted the vampire in the air and threw him mercilessly to the ground. Aryk, quick to counter picked up Angelique lost dagger and stabbed the Sleether in the face. The beast cried from the injury but again knocked the vampire away.

Out of ideas and overpowered, Aryk relied on his undead agility. The vampire somersaulted over the beast head. He landed silently behind the Sleether; Aryk wrapped his arms around the monster and held him with all his might. The hold was quickly broken and the vampire was pinned to the ground. The Sleether quickly sank his fangs in to the vampire's shoulder.

"FUCK!" the vampire screamed. The venom of a Sleether coursed through Aryk's system; luckily being a vampire gave Aryk a little resistance to the poison. Aryk could sense his already dwarfed strength being depleted due to the toxins that invaded his system.

The Sleether open its mouth slowly and ominously, Aryk could feel the hot air collide against his dead skin. Film and venom dripped over his ruby lips. The gaping mouth of creature was so enormous; Aryk's entire head could fit in the monster's waiting mouth and the Tribal Man had every intention on consuming him whole.

Knowing that if Aryk would die they would be next, Beth cried out. "Scott, shoot the urn!"

Scott dove for the shotgun that sat on the floor; he cocked and aimed. Scott attempted to shoot the urn with his weapon but it was out of bullets. Quick thinking, Scott removed his nine millimeter from his ankle and fired one bullet into the urn breaking it and it's magic. The magic that bound the Sleethers to the earthly realm was shattered. The remaining infant Sleethers were again banished from this realm and the Tribal Man lost his invulnerability.

"NA!" The beast screamed after the urn was shattered.

Aryk knew that the Tribal Man was stripped of his invincibility. Aryk, quick to capitalize, bites the Sleether in his hand. The Sleether recoils his from the vampire's bite; the blood of the Sleether had a vile taste to Aryk. With his one free hand Aryk punches the monster through its mouth exiting though the top his skull.

Dark ink blood coated his hand; Aryk used that last bit of his vigor to push the creature's corpse off of him. Aryk laid on the floor spent from his battle. The magic now broken the Sleether disintegrate; his once fleshy body began rapidly to rot and wither into a dry cadaver.

Aryk was poisoned by the blood and bite of the Sleether. The vampire's vision became obscured before he began to cough up blood. "Scott, I – I … blood"

"I bet you're really proud," Beth said in a low tone. "That was cute."

"I – I …" the vampire coughed again violently, "I always leave an impression."

"Wanna see something *cuter*," Beth said with a devilish grin. "And I'm sure you will appreciate this." Beth dug into her back pocket and pulled a folded piece of parchment paper, she glided towards him with a dark glee. Beth leaned over and lifted the discarded dagger.

"What are you doing?" Scott asked before rising to his feet.

"It's ok, Scott," Beth assured. "Everything will be ok."

Beth slid the blade across her hand causing a small superficial cut. Instantly Aryk's fangs appeared at the smell of blood, before a drop appeared Aryk could smell the metallic blood. She allowed the blood to drop on Aryk's face as he lapped the small drops.

"You like that?" Beth asked rhetorically. "Then you will love this." Beth brought the paper to her face and began to read:

"Baron, papa moun ki mouri a,
soti,
Mare viktim mwen an plas."

Aryk awoken to the smell of dirt and darkness; something was wrong, he could not move his body at all. "Scott," he called out. *That bitch,* Aryk thought. It had to be magic. "Scott," Aryk exclaimed.

"I hear you," Scott replied. His eyes focused into the darkness of night.

"What is the meaning of this?" Aryk again attempted to move from his bed of dirt. "I can't move."

"You have been bound to that specific area," Beth said. "I'll make sure I thank Angelique when I see her for this idea. Gotta appreciate Haitian Voodoo. Magic, isn't that a weakness for *vampires*?"

"You fucking, *cunt*" Aryk said with a growl.

"You KILLED Cecil," Scott screamed. "You murdered my sister. And you made me –" Scott stopped himself, he did not want to expose himself. But not to Aryk, Aryk already understood the connection. He wanted to conceal himself from Beth.

"I'm sorry Scott," Aryk said, barely able to focus due to the poison being still in his system. "I should have killed you too."

Scott was crushed; the mystical link still bound Scott to Aryk. As much as he wanted to hate Aryk and end his existence he could not. His loyalty was still with Aryk; but that was the vampire in Scott telling him that. The human side wanted revenge.

"Well no one's going to die, not even you," Scott said. "You're going to rot here, you demonic, sociopathic, piece of shit."

"Magic won't hold me forever," Aryk promised.

"As long as I'm alive," Beth said cockily.

"Oh *dear*," Aryk said with a dark drawl to his voice. The Dead Thing left the traitorous couple with a prophecy, "Then I imagine it won't be very long at all, my dear girl." Aryk gives Beth a horrifyingly charming wink, "Be seeing you both *very* soon."

The threat sent chills through Beth. Aryk could see the horror in Beth's eyes, but Beth would not allow Aryk to have the last laugh. "Thanks for the heads up; hope you enjoy your coffin, prick." Beth slams the coffin shut and climbed out of the grave she and Scott dug.

The couple then picked up their own shovels and buried the vampire. They piled the dirt on Aryk as he laughed to himself maniacally. This was not over, regardless of what the mortals believe.

Scott and Beth watched the rising sun break over the trees. The foliage began to glow a beautiful gold; and Beth reached over to Scott's hand. The shining sun glittered off Beth beautifully dirty face. She reached over a planted a soft kiss on Scott's lips.

The two walked off into the sunrise leaving Aryk to rot away in his inescapable tomb.

Fin.

#Ominous: Book Two

12.12.12

www.ingramcontent.com/pod-product-compliance
Lightning Source LLC
Chambersburg PA
CBHW022117170626
46808CB00002B/758